Bobbi + Paul
For Good
and the rem-
of Good Tim
Love
Norma

Dear John

Norma L. Betz

authorHOUSE®

AuthorHouse™
1663 Liberty Drive, Suite 200
Bloomington, IN 47403
www.authorhouse.com
Phone: 1-800-839-8640

© 2008 Norma L. Betz. All rights reserved.

No part of this book may be reproduced, stored in a retrieval system, or transmitted by any means without the written permission of the author.

First published by AuthorHouse 1/22/2008

ISBN: 978-1-4343-1071-2 (sc)

Library of Congress Control Number: 2007903030

Printed in the United States of America
Bloomington, Indiana

This book is printed on acid-free paper.

ACKNOWLEDGEMENTS

I owe a great deal of gratitude and thanks to so many people who have helped me along this literary path. In the beginning, I thought I would be able to achieve my task with a minimum of help from others. However, every step of the way, from research, writing, editing to layout and completion, required advice and help from an assortment of talented professionals and friends, each one knowledgeable in his or her own particular area. I have discovered how truly blessed I am to know such wonderful people.

My greatest debt is to my husband, Allen. His support and love through this process has enabled me to write this book. He has truly been "my dearest friend" throughout all of this and for the last forty years of our marriage.

Professor of History David Bramhall will never know how much I appreciate his calm in the midst of my internal storm to complete this project, which began as my doctoral dissertation. Dr. Bramhall made me believe all was possible and to take it one step at a time and one day at a time. His guidance through my writing and his knowledge of John Adams were invaluable.

No one can get through the process of writing without a great editor. Five years ago on a trip to Ireland, I met Virginia Duetsch, a professional editor who since has become a consultant on this project. In the short span of eleven days we began a friendship that I know will last a lifetime. Virginia's honesty kept me on track and encouraged me to question phrasing and consider other viewpoints.

Officer Matthew Ralicki of the Wanaque Police Department guided me with his expertise in police matters. An invaluable source, he helped me through the crime scenes and with the terminology necessary to make the story credible. Any errors in this area are mine, not his.

To all the veterinarians I have used in the last forty years, and especially my present veterinarian, who wishes to remain anonymous, thank you. I appreciate the time and the help with the technical scenes.

To each of my family and friends who endured the last few years with me, thank you for your infinite patience, kindness and sense of humor. There is a quote by Charles Haddon Spurgeon that was written about friends, but I think it applies to family as well:

> *Friendship is one of the sweetest*
> *joys of life. Many might have failed*
> *beneath the bitterness of their trial*
> *had they not found a friend.*

Last, but by no means least, I thank "my dearest little friend," Toby*, my faithful companion, who, through all the research, writing and completion, stayed by my side. It didn't matter what time of day or for how long, he was always there. The character of Quincy was based on Toby, and anyone who has a Weimaraner will be able to relate to this precious sidekick. His unconditional love got me through the worst times.

---

*Unfortunately, I lost my dearest little friend in January, 2006. He was almost 11 years old. In June of the same year, a new Weimaraner puppy, Quincy, joined our family. His presence has helped us heal and get through our loss.

For

My Dearest Friend

whose support and love made this all possible

Dear John

Chapter 1

Susanna Abigail Smith was dreading the trip to Weymouth. Graduation was over, yet she was not looking forward to her time off.

The end of May was always a slow time in her office. This particular Monday, she was doing everything she could to talk herself out of going to Massachusetts. Unfortunately, Quincy, the recipient of her discourse, couldn't help her make a decision. Quincy was a five-year-old Grey Weimaraner with soulful amber eyes. Susanna couldn't have a more loyal or loving friend. Not only did Quincy adore his mistress, he felt anything she said was wonderful, and anywhere she was going would be a glorious adventure.

The object of Quincy's affection was five feet eight inches, blonde, blue eyed, and struggled to keep her weight down but really needed to shed only ten pounds. Her downfall was Krispy Kreme doughnuts, which she ate only when she was stressed, like now. She had a beautiful smile, when she smiled. It was her eyes, however, that were magnetic. If it is true that the eyes are windows into the soul, then these eyes reflected a beautiful spirit.

Sitting at the kitchen table with three of the six doughnuts gone, Susanna was stroking Quincy's head, neck and ears, trying to explain why this was really a bad time to leave the office and lamenting "why me"? Quincy, on the other hand, while listening attentively, was really hoping that one of those doughnuts was coming his way. He was a little big for his breed and had sampled Krispy Kreme doughnuts before.

In Susanna's hands was a letter from the law firm of Akers, Shaw and Whitney explaining the bequests of her late aunt, Susanna Abigail Smith. Susanna had been named for her aunt. She had always hated her old-fashioned name and, especially, being the butt of jokes. Taunted with the song, "Oh Susanna" and the nickname "Suzy Q," she wished her parents had named her something more modern, like Brittany or Tiffany. Her parents, however, had wanted to carry on the historical family tradition and were thrilled when they had a daughter to carry on the name Susanna like her aunt and grandmother before her.

Susanna Abigail Smith was a direct descendant of Abigail Smith Adams, the wife of John Adams, second president of the United States. Her family history was weighty, and Susanna had always tried to ignore her famous ancestor.

But now that her aunt was dead, she had to face her family's heritage by going to Weymouth to settle her aunt's estate. This was the subject of her ramblings to Quincy, and why Susanna resisted the trip. Her aunt had left Susanna her whole estate, which included an historical family home in Weymouth and all the effects contained therein. A decision had to be made concerning these bequests. More than a year had passed since her aunt's death, and the law firm needed Susanna to come to Weymouth and sign the necessary documents to close out the estate. Included with the documents they sent was a letter from her aunt to be forwarded to Susanna in the event of her death. It was this letter that was causing the most anguish of all.

As a child, Susanna was not very close to her aunt, who lived in Massachusetts. Susanna lived in New Jersey with her parents. Her mother was an only child and her father had only one sister, the elder Susanna. Susanna's father, originally from Weymouth, was a history professor at a private independent college in Robertson, a small town in northern New Jersey. While only a few hours traveling time separated her small family, Susanna saw her aunt only on special holidays or family occasions, such as Christmas and graduations. These few events were not enough for Susanna to establish strong ties with her aunt.

Susanna and her family had lived unremarkable lives and seemed like any "happy American family." She had graduated from high school and went on to attend Rutgers University. When she was nineteen and a sophomore in college, her life took an eventful turn.

On a stormy March weekend, her father and mother were traveling back home from an educational conference in Washington, D.C. A drunk driver crossed the divide on the New Jersey Turnpike and hit her parent's car head on, killing them both instantly. Orphaned, with no other immediate family, Susanna clung to her namesake in an attempt to try to cope with her horrific loss. Aunt Susanna took control and made sure that the younger Susanna finished college and went on to graduate school. She gave love, financial support and moral advice.

In the last few years, there had been a distance between them that had been mostly geographic. What was causing so much distress now was guilt, guilt that Susanna had not been there when her aunt needed her, and that her aunt had died with no one there to comfort her. To go to her house in Weymouth would only stir up old memories and more guilt.

The letter from Aunt Susanna remained unopened. The handwriting on the envelope was familiar and reassuring, evoking memories of a warm, loving summer years before, a summer when loss and heartbreak were healed by a caring heart. A summer when they shared so much, even a trip to Cape Cod.

"Quincy, it looks like I have to stop procrastinating and take care of business."

With a sadness that was overwhelming, Susanna slit the envelope and removed the sheets of paper. Along with the letter, a key fell from the envelope.

My Darling Susanna

If you are reading this, then the cancer I fought with all my might has won. I am sorry we didn't get together last summer but I know how crazy your job is especially in the summer and how difficult it is for you to get away. You are now totally on your own and for that I am sorry. Family is important and, while you like your independence, hopefully you will come to realize the need to have this connection. I have left you the house in Weymouth as well its contents in the desire that you will find the roots and security you need. Of course, I hope you will keep the house, but you are free to do with it what you will. Take your time and make the right decision. I have enclosed the key for your use. Remember your historical heritage and realize the value it has in your life.

I will be watching over you, as have your parents. Know you were loved and that the few short years we had together were precious to me.

Love,

Aunt Susanna

The pages fell from Susanna's hands. Tears streamed down her cheeks. The walls she had put up over the years slowly began to crumble and all the grief and sadness finally poured out. The loss of her aunt hit hard, harder than Susanna had realized. For the first time, she realized that her whole family was gone and there was no getting them back. Her determination to be independent over the years had prevented her from making more of an effort with her aunt. Susanna had let the family tie loosen.

"Quincy, there's no other decision to make. I wasn't there in the end but now I can at least do the right thing, like Aunt Susanna did for me when Mom and Dad died. How do you feel about a road trip? Let's get packed and on the way. The sooner we get this over with, the happier I will be. Let me call the office and give them a number in case they need me, and then let's call Mrs. O'Hara and ask her to watch the house for us."

Susanna was a financial aid director at the same college where her father had taught. She had held her position for five years and was very good at her job. Her only fault was that she needed to delegate more responsibilities and let her staff do their jobs.

It wasn't that she felt they couldn't do the job, it was her internal need to constantly be the best and prove herself. If she were a fly on the wall, she would have seen that her staff was really happy when she was out of the office. Although they loved her and wouldn't want any other boss, periodically they needed a break and were delighted when she called to tell them she would be out of town for two weeks.

Mrs. O'Hara, on the other hand, was not happy. Born in Ireland sixty-five years before, she had arrived in America at age twelve and, despite her American education, she had never lost her sweet, lilting Irish accent. She was widowed young with no children, and she became attached to Susanna ten years ago when she moved next door. She thought of Susanna as if she were her own daughter and was fiercely protective of her.

"Ah, Darlin', you have had enough hurt. Let the lawyers take care of it for you."

"I can't do that Mrs. O'Hara. I have to do the right thing and that's doing it in person. I'll only be gone for two weeks. I'll put the house up there for sale and I'll sell the contents. I just need to get started and put it in the hands of a capable real estate agent. Once all that's done I will come home and get on with my life. I might need to go back and finalize things, but it will be easier for me to do that later when I'm not so emotional. So, please, watch the house for me and take in my mail, and if you remember, water the plants that I have been trying to kill."

"I will take care of everything for you, but I have this feeling, a premonition if you will, that something is going to happen. Please do be careful. I don't like this at all, at all. If you need me, anytime, anytime at all, call me."

Quincy watched his mistress put down the telephone and put that worried look on his face. He knew something was going on and that his mistress was sad, but he also knew that she was going out and she wasn't leaving him behind. When Susanna placed his blanket by the garage door, Quincy always felt it a wise move to place himself squarely between the blanket and the garage door thereby eliminating any possibility of being left behind. Since he weighed a hundred pounds, there was very little likelihood of anybody getting by him.

In a short time, the Dodge Durango was filled with clothes, dog food, biscuits, dog bed, assorted bottles of water, Krispy Kremes and, of course, Quincy. Susanna, who should have known the way, had always been directionally challenged, and was now hunched over a map of the northeast United States.

"Quincy, it looks like we need to take Route 287 North to Interstate 95 and follow the signs to Boston. Weymouth is south of Boston and, as we get closer, we will have to wing it from memory or stop and ask for directions. Are you game?"

Quincy, true to his breed, licked Susanna's face as if to say, "I'm game for anything you are."

With their seatbelts in place, Susanna drove out of the driveway, hoping this would all be over soon so they could get back to their routine. What she could not know was that Mrs. O'Hara's premonition would come to pass. Their lives would change forever. Nothing would ever be the same.

Chapter 2

"Quincy, there is something to be said about living in New Jersey. At least when you stop at a gas station, they pump gas for you.

"This is a nightmare. Not only do I have trouble with directions, I can't even pump my own gas. Just be thankful you're a dog and you don't have to be embarrassed and ask somebody how to fill a gas tank. Good Lord, it's unbelievable that someone with an advanced degree can't figure this out."

With that, Susanna went to a cubicle that looked like Fort Knox and saw inside a young man of about twenty-two, with a shaved head and God knows how many tattoos, sitting, reading a magazine. She knocked on the Plexiglas. The young man looked up, startled that anyone would disturb him.

"Sir, do you think you can help me, I don't know how to work the pump."

"Geez, lady, everybody knows how to do that."

"I realize many people know how to do this. I don't. Where I come from, we don't pump our own gas."

"Why didn't you say you're from Jersey in the first place? I'll be right out."

With this humiliating experience over and the gas paid for, Susanna was on the road again.

"Quincy, let's hope this gas lasts until we get there. I'm going to have to learn how to do this or we will never get back home. We should probably think about eating, too. Let's drive for another hour and we'll find a good place to chow down, maybe Burger King?" Quincy agreed—he was never one to refuse a meal.

After five hours, several wrong turns, and many stops to ask for directions, Susanna and Quincy finally pulled into the driveway in front of her late aunt's house. It was just as Susanna remembered it, a white, saltbox-style colonial, dating back to the 1700s. The house had been upgraded over the centuries and was actually quite cozy. Her aunt had done a remarkable job updating while not destroying the historical look of the home. As Susanna sat in her car staring at the house, memories rushed back to her. Aunt Susanna had told her about the history of the house and, as she sat in front of it, those familiar stories came back to her.

The house, as old as it was, remained inviting and charming. The frame was hewn from oak trees that had grown on the property and was constructed with the help of most of the townspeople. Its design was medieval as most British homes were of that day. (1) Originally, it was just a two-story house. To give it the characteristics of the saltbox, as it is called today, a lean-to addition with a sloping roof was added across the rear of the house. Later generations had painted the house white, and Susanna's aunt had kept it that way. She refused to change the color, believing it should stay as true to its original state as possible. Aunt Susanna had also landscaped the property to enhance the magnificent oak trees and had added an unattached garage and driveway to complete the picture.

(1)see chapter notes

The house was actually very close in distance to the birthplace of Abigail Adams, whose family was prominent in the town of Weymouth. As a descendent of Abigail Adams, Aunt Susanna had been able to list the house in the Historical Society's Register. Susanna's aunt was always mindful of the historical significance of her home and tried to maintain its integrity. The house, for its age, was in very good condition.

"Well, Quincy, let's go inside."

Quincy was happy to get out of the car and run around for a bit. While he loved riding in the car, five hours was a long time. Using his hunter's nose to sniff every spot, Quincy was sure he smelled many scents that reminded him of his own backyard. He was all set to check them out when his mistress called him back.

"Let's unpack the car, get you some water, and find a place for your bowls. Here, hold on to your leash."

Susanna opened the front door with the key from the envelope and stepped back in time to a summer many years ago.

The house had not changed. The parlor on the left contained many of her aunt's needlepoint pieces and subtle touches. The furniture was placed as she remembered. Even the photos on the piano were the same. What was uncanny was the lingering fragrance of lavender, her aunt's favorite perfume. It was as if her aunt were out for the day and would return any minute. Susanna looked up at the door expecting to see her there, tall, proud, with her beautiful, shiny chestnut-colored hair.

"I wonder if her hair turned gray in the end. I should have come. I should have been here."

Aunt Susanna's image stayed with Susanna and a longing enveloped her to turn back the years and see not only her aunt but also her mother and father again. Susanna might have stayed in this nostalgic mood, but for the yelp that emanated from the kitchen.

"Quincy! Oh my, what have you gotten into?"

Susanna ran to the back of the house to the huge kitchen and found Quincy lying down on the floor licking his front left paw. Susanna sat down next to him and took hold of the injured paw, only to discover a small needle sticking out of the pad. She removed the needle and checked the paw to make sure there wasn't any real damage. Rubbing his head and ears to soothe him, she could see everything looked okay.

"It's okay boy, no harm."

Quincy, happy, licked both sides of his mistress's face as if to say thank you.

"Quincy, Aunt Susanna was forever losing these needles when she did her needlepoint. I'm going to have to check the house out to see if she dropped anymore, but until I do, please keep your paws and nose out of trouble."

The kitchen was Susanna's favorite room in the house. It had a large fireplace in the center, a cozy sitting area on one end, and a corner eating nook with cushions covered with blue and white gingham. The eating nook looked out onto the backyard, where a group of peach and pear trees grew. Mighty oaks shaded the small gazebo where her aunt had sat, weather permitting, to do needlepoint or read. Off to the right of the kitchen counter and refrigerator was a huge pantry, still stocked with canned peaches and pears and other staples put up in case of heavy snows. The room was not modern by any means, but it was comfortable and felt like home.

"Quincy, after I get us set up, let's go explore the town and get some supplies. Tomorrow I'll have to go see the lawyers and try to get the ball rolling on the closing of the estate, so tonight let's try to get you some exercise."

Chapter 3

The Weymouth town founders would have been pleased with the character that present day Weymouth retained. Established in 1622 as Wessagusset, the town was renamed Weymouth in 1635 and is the second largest, oldest town in the Commonwealth of Massachusetts. Simple houses and churches that were wooden replicas of the brick and stone architecture of European origin had graced the original town. Some survived as reminders of this past. Weymouth and the surrounding towns were witnesses to and their inhabitants participants in the American Revolution.

Although it thrived as a seaport, the town had been connected to nearby communities by a simple network of paths and roads that had found the most convenient routes through varied upland terrain. The skeletal remains of the early roadway network could still be traced in some of the town's streets and ways. A meandering pattern of main roads enhanced the charm of the town. (2) It was this approximate seventeen miles of history that Susanna and Quincy explored.

The decision to stop at present day Great Esker Park was thoroughly approved by Quincy, who never lost an opportunity to run and check out all the scents in new territory.

Hiking trails were right up Quincy's alley but not Susanna's. She had a tendency to let the desire to exercise pass her right by. But she knew that Quincy needed to run, so she was willing to give up her inertia to keep him healthy. After about an hour, she had had it.

"Quincy, let's go. It's time for dinner and some food shopping. Let's find a grocery store and a place for take-out. What do you feel like? How about that chicken place we passed on the way here? You, of course, will have your regular food, but perhaps one or two French fries will come your way. In the car with you!"

Quincy was always obedient where food was concerned, so he quickly jumped into the front seat and patiently waited for Susanna to drive away.

After the chicken was consumed and Quincy fed and walked for the last time, Susanna was ready to go upstairs, unpack and get some sleep. She climbed the stairs as she had done before, but this time it was different. There was a lonely, almost eerie feeling that she had never felt before. She couldn't bring herself to look into her aunt's bedroom.

"There will be time to do that," she said out loud. "Time to face the past."

With that thought, she turned to her right and went into the bedroom that had been hers long ago. As with the parlor, nothing had been changed. Everything was as she had left it. She placed Quincy's bed alongside her four-poster bed and lay down on top of the covers.

"Tomorrow is another day."

The trip and the emotions of the day had exhausted her, and within minutes she was sound asleep with Quincy snoring loudly on his blanket beside her.

At ten o'clock the next morning Susanna was in the reception area of the Akers, Shaw and Whitney law office awaiting her appointment with senior partner James Shaw.

A prestigious, old law firm, Akers, Shaw and Whitney had been in business for more than fifty years. The office exuded that established confidence that only years of success can achieve. Susanna was pondering how her aunt could afford such expensive legal services when Mr. Shaw's assistant, Holly, came into the room and escorted her to his office.

Not normally impressed with furnishings or surroundings, Susanna was almost speechless when she entered Mr. Shaw's office. What awed Susanna most was the expanse of the room. It was immense, with wall-to-wall, ceiling-to-floor mahogany bookcases, filled with the usual law reference books and annotated codes but also with historical books of all types. In between two arched windows sat an antique desk also made of mahogany and a burgundy leather chair from which a very handsome, statesman-like, gray-haired gentleman was rising.

"Miss Smith, my name is James Shaw and it is a great pleasure to finally meet you. Your aunt spoke of you often, and I am happy to say you are just as she described you. Please come in, sit down, and make yourself comfortable."

Susanna was a little perplexed but proceeded to sit in one of the high-backed leather chairs facing the desk.

"I'm afraid I'm at a slight disadvantage, I had no idea my aunt even had a lawyer until you sent that first letter almost a year ago. Did you know her well?" she inquired.

"Your Aunt Susanna and I were great friends as well as lawyer and client. We were actually childhood sweethearts. We drifted apart when we both went to college, and met other people. I married, your aunt did not. I should have married her, for you see, I discovered too late that I truly loved her. My marriage ended in divorce after twenty-five years. Ten years ago your aunt and I met by accident at the Hare and Tortoise Restaurant. She was having dinner with friends, and I walked in with a client. She hadn't changed. I knew her instantly. We agreed to meet for lunch the next day and saw each other very often after that until her death last year."

Susanna was trying to take all this in. This was a side to her aunt that she didn't know. In all the years she thought she knew her aunt, nothing was ever mentioned about men, let alone a mature romantic relationship. But then, she had not really visited much in the last 10 years. She hadn't even made it to the funeral. By the time she had learned of her aunt's death, it was too late. Her aunt had already been buried. Susanna was stunned by his revelation. Would there be more to come?

"I see I have surprised you. Please forgive me. I am rambling like an old fool. I just need you to know how special your aunt was to me and how much I mourn her passing. For ten years, she gave me back a life I thought was gone forever and, if you will, a second chance. I also want you to know what your aunt wanted for you and what I promised I would do to try to make these wishes come true.

"Are you all right? Can I get something? Coffee? Tea? Water? Cookies?"

Susanna was trying to digest all this information and for once in her life was speechless.

All she could say was, "Coffee would be great."

Never one to let food pass her by in a crisis she added, "And maybe a cookie."

James Shaw called to Holly and requested that she bring in the coffee and cookies. There was a stillness in the room until the tray arrived. After Holly left, Susanna finally found her voice.

"Mr. Shaw, I must tell you how surprised I am by this information. My aunt never mentioned you. This is the first time I'm hearing about any of this. I must also tell you that I'm happy my aunt had companionship and that someone was with her at the end. I'm here, however, to settle the estate, and I must get it done quickly so that I can return home and get back to my office. Can we please get down to the business at hand?"

Mr. Shaw looked at Susanna sadly, and for a moment it appeared as if he were going to say something, but he stopped himself and, in an instant, was the polished lawyer he had always been. What Susanna didn't realize was how difficult the confession had been for this proud man. He had always kept his emotions close to the vest and had never opened up to anyone like this, not even his son. The moment passed and all he could say was, "As you wish."

"Your aunt lived comfortably on the pension from her position as librarian at the local town library and from her Social Security. She never made an enormous amount of money, but she did enjoy her work and truly had a happy life. At the time of her death, she had accumulated fifty thousand dollars in investments, CDs, and so on, as well as a twenty-five thousand dollar life insurance policy. She owned the house in Weymouth outright and, of course, there were her possessions. She made me the executor of her will, so I took care of all her debts and funeral expenses.

"She also had some specific bequests. Ten-thousand dollars was to go to the library to be used to purchase equipment necessary to keep it updated; ten-thousand was to go to the local Historical Society to be used for archival maintenance; and lastly, ten thousand was to go to her alma mater to set up a scholarship fund for history majors. The remainder of her money was to go to you, as well as the house and its contents. The final accounting after costs leaves you with thirty-two thousand dollars in cash and the house and contents. I have the accounting sheets for you and the deed to the house. It is your decision as to what you want to do with these items. Do you have any questions?"

Susanna was stunned by her aunt's bequests—she knew about the house and contents, but had no idea about the money!

"I didn't realize that Aunt Susanna had any money. She was always so frugal, and I always felt it was difficult for her.

I'm overwhelmed. I need to let this information sink in, before I decide what to do.

"If I do decide to sell the house, do you know a real estate agent I can use?"

"My son is a broker and has his own firm. I can recommend him, and not because he's my son but because he's good. Here's his business card if you decide to sell. I must tell you however, that your aunt requested two more things of me. The first thing was the letter I sent to you. The other is to tell you about another letter she left for you at her home. She asked that you read it before you decide anything. It's on top of the family antique trunk in her bedroom.

"Well, I have fulfilled my professional duty to your aunt. Should you need help or have any further questions, please don't hesitate to contact me."

"Thank you Mr. Shaw for all your help. I will need to review everything and then I will let you know what I decide."

Susanna got up from the chair, collected the estate documents and proceeded to walk out the door.

"Miss Smith, please take your time. Don't make any rash decisions. Your aunt really wanted you to have the house. It has been in your family for over two-hundred years."

"I will take my time, Mr. Shaw. Goodbye."

As James Shaw watched her leave the room, he wondered about this young woman. She certainly did not have the warmth and gentle nature of her aunt, but there was a similar vulnerability that they had in common. This woman was aloof. Her aunt was not. Maybe he had divulged too much of his personal feelings, but he had felt so comfortable with his Susanna's niece. Perhaps he should hold his judgment until he knew her better.

Susanna looked at her watch when she left and discovered it was twelve-thirty. Quincy had been in the car for over two hours, and she needed to get back to him

Happy as always to see her, Quincy sensed that something had happened.

"Hi sweetheart, how have you been? I know. It's been a long time, but I will make it up to you."

Reaching in her pocket for her keys, Susanna found the business card for Mr. Shaw's son: Shaw's Realty, John Shaw, Broker. She pondered what to do for a few minutes, and then reached for her cell phone.

"Good afternoon. Shaw Realty. How may I direct your call?"

Susanna noticed the telephone receptionist had the typical Boston accent and wondered if she was a transplant from that city.

"May I speak to John Shaw, please?"

"May I ask who is calling?" inquired the receptionist.

"Please tell him it's Susanna Smith, and I am calling on behalf of my late aunt, Susanna Smith."

"Please hold the line."

"John Shaw here, how may I help you Miss Smith?"

"Mr. Shaw, I have just come from your father's office. He gave me your business card and suggested I give you a call in regard to my aunt's house. I inherited her home in Weymouth, and I'm thinking of putting the house on the market. Would you be able to meet me at the house tomorrow and give me an appraisal?"

"I could meet you at ten o'clock if that's convenient."

"That would be fine. Let me give you the address."

"No need. I know where the house is. I've been there before. You see, I knew your aunt very well. She was a favorite of mine, and of all the school children in Weymouth who remember her from the library. She always found time for us.

"Well, I'll see you tomorrow at ten."

The phone clicked in Susanna's ear before she could respond. She thought how little she really knew about her aunt and how much she was finding out. She wondered if she was doing the right thing by selling the house.

"Quincy, why do I feel so bad about all of this? Aunt Susanna said I could do what I want with the house. I have to sell it. My life is in New Jersey, not Weymouth."

With these thoughts, Susanna pulled away from the law offices and headed back to the house. She needed to walk Quincy and she also needed to have lunch.

She felt confused. Maybe things would be in sharper focus after a meal. Perhaps then she could face her demons and look through the house and get it ready for sale. She needed to decide what she would keep and what she would need to get rid of.

"Yes, Quincy, after your walk and lunch we we'll deal with these things."

The trip back was uneventful, and Quincy was happy to go for his walk. After lunch, Susanna started an inventory of her aunt's house, beginning with the parlor.

Susanna was drawn to the photographs on top of the lace shawl on the piano. For the first time, she really looked at the pictures in the frames. There was a photo of Aunt Susanna as a young woman, perhaps in her early twenties. Next to this was one of her parents' wedding. They were so young and were such a handsome couple. Susanna saw that she looked very much like her mother but had her father's height and frame. Assorted other photos were arranged as if in a time line. Susanna's baby picture, grammar school and high school pictures, both college and graduate school graduations and, finally, a snapshot of Susanna and her aunt, taken at Cape Cod that sad summer.

Positioned behind these frames was an old, posed photo of a young man, a portrait in the style of a studio photograph taken back in the late forties or early fifties. There was something familiar about the face, and suddenly Susanna realized that it was James Shaw.

"Why didn't I ever see this before! She really did know him well. She must have really loved him. Why else would she keep his picture with everyone else she loved? The question is, why didn't she marry him after his divorce? They could have had ten great years together as husband and wife. And why didn't she tell me about him?"

The thought that she should ask Mr. Shaw when she saw him again passed through her mind and quickly left when she realized that it would be an invasion of his privacy. She also thought that she had been too short with him today.

"Maybe I should explain things to him. Maybe tell him how hard all this is for me. How guilty I feel for not being there for Aunt Susanna. I have to tell him the next time I see him. What must he think of me?"

She would have to keep the photos, of course, perhaps ask Mr. Shaw if he would like his picture back.

"I think he would like that. I wonder what else I should keep."

Turning around, she looked at the comfortable chair in the corner next to the antique bookcase. She pictured her aunt sitting there reading books and remembered her passion for early American history. The books in the bookcase reflected this interest and enthusiasm for her heritage as well, for there were also many books on the Adams family. Prolific letter and diary writers, they were well represented as their works took up most of the bookcase. Susanna thought that she would have to keep the books as well.

"Quincy, this is not going to be easy. So far I can't get rid of anything. I have a feeling this is going to take a lot longer than I thought."

Sitting down in the chair, Susanna felt weary. Quincy came over and sat down next to her, leaned in and raised his head upward hoping to get his chin and neck rubbed. At the same time, he gave comfort to his mistress. Susanna put her hand down automatically and touched his head. They were very much a team and knew each other's habits well.

She reached over and took down a book of letters between John Adams and Thomas Jefferson and began to read. Before she knew it, it was seven thirty in the evening, and Quincy was starting to give her his paw, which meant it was past time to eat.

"Okay, okay. Keep your fur on. I'll get your dinner. You know, it wouldn't hurt you to miss a meal." Quincy, as if knowing what she said, gave her a look.

"I know. It wouldn't hurt me either. C'mon let's get you and me fed."

After dinner, Susanna went upstairs. She felt it was time to go into her aunt's bedroom and read the letter that Mr. Shaw said was left for her. It was there, right where he said it would be, on top of the antique chest. Susanna picked up the envelope and noticed her name in the familiar handwriting. Sitting in the rocker, Susanna held the envelope in her hand, afraid to open it, afraid that she would not be able to do whatever her aunt would ask of her, and yet knowing she must.

My Darling Susanna,

By now you have met with James Shaw and know the contents of my will. I hope you are happy with my decisions. I know you, perhaps better than you know yourself, and am aware that you will probably want to sell the house and all its contents. You never wanted to get close to anyone after your parents died and put up so many barriers. I also know you loved me in your own way and that I was a poor substitute for your parents. What you are not aware of is your need to have roots and family. You would like everyone to think of you as a free, independent woman who never gets emotionally involved, who keeps a cool head, and is in control at all times. The truth, however, is that you are very insecure and when in trouble use self-deprecating humor to detach yourself. You are a wonderful young woman, and you brought much joy into my life. I want to do the same for you.

I am going to ask you to do some things for me. First, I would like you to take your time in making the decision whether or not to sell the house. I believe this house will give you the roots and security you need. Second, I need you to review the contents of the trunk on which you found this letter. There are family letters that may help you to realize the value of your heritage and you may even uncover a family secret. These letters are valuable, more valuable then money itself, as they have been in the family for over two hundred years.

Lastly, I want you to listen to James Shaw. He is a wonderful man and will only look out for your best interests. He has been a true friend to me and has helped me throughout the years. Don't shut him out. He will need your support and comfort as well.

This is it, my darling. Please be happy. Find someone to love, have children, and live your life.

All my love,

Aunt Susanna

Guilt is funny. It makes you think and do things you ordinarily wouldn't, or so thought Susanna as she finished her aunt's letter. Fighting with her own emotions and debating whether to cancel her appointment with John Shaw the next morning, Susanna was brought back to her senses by Quincy's paw touching her knee. Quincy didn't have a sensitive light touch, so when he touched her it got her attention.

"Oh boy, I guess you need a walk. I think this is a good idea. Maybe it will clear my head. Okay, Quincy let's get your leash."

The night air was refreshing. May can be tricky, Susanna thought. Sometimes it's cold with no hint of spring, other times it's warm and cozy with a touch of renewal in the air, as it was this night.

At any other time or place, Susanna would have relished this time with Quincy. Tonight it was only therapeutic for her. Fighting demons of her own making and trying to make decisions, she walked Quincy for over an hour. By the time they came back to the house, Susanna knew what she must do. She would read the letters since it seemed so important to her aunt that she do so, and she would keep the appointment with John Shaw the next morning. After that she would decide the future of the house.

The rest of the night she spent taking inventory of the house and getting familiar with what was there. When the antique grandfather clock bonged twelve midnight, it was time to go to bed and finish the task in the morning. Within minutes, Quincy was snoring loudly. As she was fading into sleep, Susanna thought how warm and comfy the old house was, and she was surprised at how right it felt to be there.

Chapter 4

At precisely ten in the morning, John Shaw pulled up in front of the house. He drove a Jeep Cherokee that looked like it had seen better days. Susanna pondered this and wondered if he really was as good and successful as his father said he was. The metropolitan area in which she lived had influenced her conception of what real estate agents should be. Those agents looked slick, drove a Mercedes or Lincoln and were always pushing for a deal. John Shaw certainly didn't have that image. When the car door opened and he stepped out, Susanna was a little surprised. John Shaw was a younger version of his father. In fact, he could have been the young man in the photograph on the piano. Both of the Shaw's could have been Hollywood leading men. She was amazed at the strong resemblance both of them had to the actor James Brolin.

This is going to be interesting, thought Susanna, as she held Quincy by the collar. Quincy loved people. It was hard to get into the house without being licked to death. Susanna usually held his collar until any guests were firmly established within her residence. Once John was sniffed and licked, Quincy would calm down and behave. She hoped he wasn't allergic or, worse yet, a dog hater. That could ruin their business relationship.

Dressed in tan khakis, blue polo shirt and Docksiders without socks, John Shaw was the epitome of summer cool. He was full of energy and self-assurance as he came down the path and knocked on the front door. Susanna opened the door holding onto Quincy and asked, "Are you afraid of dogs, or allergic? If so I will put him in the upstairs bedroom."

"Not at all. I love dogs. I had a Golden myself but he was diagnosed with cancer, and I had to have him put to sleep when he was 12 years old."

"I'm so sorry. Come on in. He will adjust and calm down. He might lick you, though."

John Shaw came through the door to a stub-wagging, happy dog. Quincy was allowed to sniff and eventually did calm down. He took an immediate liking to John, the kind of kinship that only comes between dogs and dog lovers. Quincy followed him around and never left his side.

"I was just going to have a cup of coffee. Would you like one?" asked Susanna.

"That would be great."

"Please come into the kitchen and sit down."

They all went into the kitchen. John Shaw and Quincy positioned themselves at the kitchen nook. Quincy all but crawled under John's skin and wanted to be petted constantly. Susanna poured coffee into two cups and placed sugar and cream on the table.

"Quincy, leave Mr. Shaw alone and come sit by me." Quincy did not budge.

"Quincy, come here! Mr. Shaw, I am truly sorry. He always behaves. I don't know what's gotten into him."

"Don't worry about it, Miss Smith. I seem to have this affect on dogs. It really doesn't bother me. Good coffee—and please, call me John."

"Thank you, and please call me Susanna."

"Susanna, what exactly would you like me to do?"

"I need you to give me an appraisal for the house, as I'm thinking about putting it up for sale. I really don't know the market value, nor do I know how quickly a house in this area will sell. I also might sell the house with some or all of the contents, so I will need to get a value on the furniture and contents as well."

"This is really a great old house. I remember coming here with my dad for dinner or sometimes lunch when I was in college. My mom and dad were divorced, and I would see my dad on occasion when I had some time off. I didn't get to see him much when I was a teenager. It wasn't exactly a friendly divorce. I think the happiest I ever saw him was when he was with your aunt. She was a truly wonderful woman."

John looked away sadly and surveyed the kitchen.

"I just love this kitchen. Can't you just imagine how it must have been two hundred years ago? This room has a peace and warmth you don't often feel in other homes."

Susanna let him ramble on. She was trying to figure him out. She thought he was nice, but there was a complexity to him that puzzled her. Susanna was also a little taken aback by the relationship that had developed between John Shaw and Quincy. If a stranger were viewing this scenario, it would look as if Quincy were John's dog, not Susanna's. While she wouldn't admit it to herself, Susanna was a little upset about this sudden affection and perhaps even a little jealous.

"Will you be able to do this?" asked Susanna. "I only have the rest of this week and next week to get things rolling. After that, I have to go back to New Jersey and my job."

"No problem. Let me take measurements today and then I'll calculate a price. I will also get in touch with an auctioneer I know, who does estate sales. He can give you a price for the contents. I'll try to get him here by the end of this week. Is that soon enough?"

"Yes, that's fine."

"Good, let me get to work then."

John Shaw got up from the chair and Quincy followed him like a lost puppy. He would have followed him right out the door, but Susanna grabbed his collar and told him to sit. Quincy, not one to hide his dislike for things, gave a look that would have wilted a flower.

"I'm sorry, but John has work to do and you have to stay out of his way."

John was very diligent and measured the square footage of each room, looked at the bathroom, checked out appliances and did virtually everything a good real estate broker should do. After he finished with the house, he looked at the outside property and used the deed and plat of the land to see the dimensions of the lot on which the house sat. When he was done, he knocked on the door.

"I have all the information I need right now and will get back to you by tomorrow with a sale price. Do you need anything else?" asked John.

"No, that will be fine. You have the house telephone number?"

"Yes, I do. Until tomorrow, have a good day."

He walked to his car and moments later drove away. Watching him go, Susanna felt a pang of guilt about selling the house. Quincy's whining only compounded this feeling of guilt. It made her wonder if she was doing the right thing.

"Quincy, what is wrong with you? You act as if you want to go with him! Stop whining. You're my dog, not his." Quincy gave up his position at the window and walked away dejected.

"Okay, come with me and let me get you a biscuit. Maybe that will make you feel better."

Never one to give up a treat, Quincy followed Susanna to the kitchen and got his tasty morsel.

"What am I going to do with you my fair-weather friend? Let's get ready to go out. I have to get some computer supplies for my laptop, and I have to pick up some groceries. Then we'll have a nice long walk and head back to the house. When we come back, we'll start reading those letters that Aunt Susanna left for me."

Before she could leave the house, Susanna's cell phone rang, playing the familiar "Can Can" music that always startled her at first. Looking at the caller ID, she saw that it was Mrs. O'Hara.

"Hi, Mrs. O'Hara. Are you okay? Is everything all right with the house?"

"Calm down, Darlin'. Everything is okay. I am just worried about you. How are you getting on with your plans?"

Susanna, relieved that there weren't any problems at home, responded, "Things are going as planned. As a matter of fact, I just had the real estate broker here. He's going to give me a quote on the house, and if it seems reasonable I'll probably let him list it."

"Make sure he is reputable and not a fly-by-night. Please protect yourself. There are a lot of shady characters out there."

"Mrs. O'Hara, he's very reputable. His name is John Shaw, and he's the son of my aunt's lawyer."

"Oh Darlin'! Is he single? Is he your age? Is he handsome? Maybe you have met your soul mate!" sputtered the romantic Mrs. O'Hara.

"Mrs. O'Hara, you are impossible. It's only business and, besides, I'll only be here for another week and a half. It's hard to start a relationship in that short period of time. I can assure you that John Shaw certainly has no interest in me other than selling the house."

"Well, we shall see. Please call me in a couple of days and let me know how you are. I do worry about you. Take care of yourself, love. Ta-Ta."

"I will call you. I promise," said Susanna.

Susanna did not know that just then John Shaw was having thoughts similar to Mrs. O'Hara's. As he drove away from the house, he was surprised at the feelings he was experiencing. What was it about Susanna Smith? She certainly wasn't the most beautiful woman he had ever met, but there was something there that intrigued him. There was something behind the wall she put up. Maybe it was the blue eyes, maybe the smile—when she did smile—or maybe it was the way she looked at Quincy.

"Susanna Smith, you are an enigma. I think I'm going to have to find out more about you," he said out loud.

Afraid someone might cart him away for talking to himself, he stopped and drove back to his office.

Chapter 5

By six o'clock, Susanna and Quincy had finished their shopping, eaten dinner and gone for a long walk. Coming back into the house, Susanna thought about the letters in the trunk. She ought to get it over with and start reading them. She was running out of time.

"Let me make a cup of tea and go upstairs."

Tea in hand, she and Quincy climbed the stairs and went into Aunt Susanna's bedroom. Susanna sat in her aunt's rocker, with Quincy lying down on the rug beside her. She opened the trunk and took out the wooden box that contained the letters. The box was old and made of oak. It was hinged and about the size of a breadbox, with a mellow luster and warmth to it, like only an antique piece can have. It was handmade and Susanna wondered who in the family had made it. Opening the box, she was surprised at the number of letters contained within it.

"Gosh, there must be ten letters here. I wonder how old they are—I'm sure that's why Aunt Susanna kept them. They appear to be in excellent condition. My guess is that they're very valuable."

Each letter had been protected by tissue paper and wrapped in cheesecloth. Attached to the top of the letters was an envelope that had yellowed with age with what appeared to be a letter inside. The envelope was addressed to Susanna Smith. From the appearance of the envelope, while newer than the other letters, she knew this envelope must be old, too.

"This must have been for Aunt Susanna, yet the handwriting looks familiar, Quincy. It almost looks like her handwriting, but not exactly the same. I guess I need to open this first before I read the others."

Carefully opening the envelope, Susanna took out the pages of the letter to read. It was addressed to Susanna's aunt. Quickly glancing at the end, Susanna discovered that her paternal grandfather, William Smith, had written the letter. Susanna's father had told her that her grandfather had been married at the age of 50 to her grandmother, who was 30 at the time. They were very happy and within a short period of time had two children. Susanna's aunt was born first and then her father two years later. When Aunt Susanna was nineteen and her father seventeen, their father passed away. He was 70 years old. It was a shock to the family, but Susanna's grandmother carried out her husband's request to raise her children well. Both of her children went on to college and to respected professions.

Susanna's grandfather had been a history teacher at the local high school and had written and researched many historical pieces. While Susanna's father had only seventeen years with his father, he always respected this gentle man who had such a passion for history. It was one of the reasons her father had become a history professor.

Susanna only knew about her grandfather through the memories of her father. Her father's memories told of a different man than his pictures showed. Every picture Susanna had seen of her grandfather portrayed a very stern looking man, stiff and unbending. Yet her father told of a loving, affectionate man, a little absent minded but gentle and caring. Susanna was sorry she never met him or her grandmother, both of whom were gone before she was born.

"Quincy, it's interesting isn't it that Aunt Susanna should lose her father at nineteen like I did. Maybe that's why she felt such anguish for me that summer. Maybe reading these letters will help me learn more about my family. There are so many missing pieces, so much I don't know. Why didn't I ask more questions when I was younger? Why did I have to lose my parents when I was so young? For the first time, I feel alone."

Susanna began to read.

June 15, 1956
My Sweet Susanna

Today is your birthday. You are eighteen and have reached a point in your life when you will soon leave the nest and go out on your own. College is only three months away and your mother and I are very proud of your accomplishments. We both know that this is only the beginning of many, and that you will achieve much in your life. The dilemma I have today is what to give you on such a special day in your life. I talked with your mother and we both have agreed on a gift. We hope you approve.

I have told you often of your family history and you certainly know your lineage, but did you know that there were letters from our most famous relative, Abigail Smith Adams? Are you also aware that in these letters there is a mystery that Abigail solves? Of course not! I am sure this comes as a surprise. Abigail Smith Adams was a remarkable woman, a woman that present day women owe a great deal to. She was the forerunner of equality in marriage, in politics, and in business, in her case running a farm. She was a prolific letter writer, and it is this body of work that has helped historians to get a good grip on what life was like in the pre-Revolutionary days up to the turn of the nineteenth century. These letters reveal a portion of the time in her life when she was duly stressed. It is how she conducts herself that is the key.

I believe you are very much like her, and it is fitting that you be the keeper of such a treasure. I know if Abigail Smith Adams were alive today she would very much approve of you and be proud to have you as a relative. I am sure she would want you to carry on the family name with pride and honor and help women to achieve their rightful places in this country. The next fifty years will see many changes and hopefully you will be a torchbearer in the area of women's rights.

Please keep these letters in the family. They are materially valuable, but have more intrinsic value than money. This is history, history that cannot be replaced nor that will have more meaning to anyone than it does the descendants of such a great woman. Family is everything. Hopefully you know that already and, if not, you will come to realize this fact. Your mother and I can think of no more fitting a gift than these letters. Cherish them. Keep them close to your heart and pass them down to your daughter as I have passed them down to mine. These letters should stay with the women in our family as a testament to the famous lady who wrote them.

Have a wonderful birthday, my sweet one.

Your loving father

"Oh Quincy, how sad. He would be dead a little more than a year later. He seemed to love her so much. No wonder Dad talked about him with such reverence. Grandfather does seem like a kind and caring soul, just like Dad said."

The ring of the telephone brought Susanna out of her thoughts and downstairs to the parlor.

"Hello, Smith residence."

"Susanna, this is John, John Shaw. I'm sorry to bother you but my auctioneer, Jerry Carter, is only free tomorrow at ten o'clock for a look at the contents of your house. Since you were in such a hurry, I thought you might want to meet with him. He's very good and also very fair. Is ten o'clock okay?"

"Tomorrow will be fine. I'll be here," she replied.

"This should only take a couple of hours. Could I take you to lunch afterwards? I know a very nice little inn not far from here that serves wonderful chowder. You might like it."

"That sounds nice, but let me think about it, and let's see how long it takes for the inventory."

"As you wish. Until tomorrow, Susanna."

Susanna hung up the phone and wondered what that was all about. John Shaw didn't seem that interested in her earlier, and now he wanted to take her to lunch.

"Maybe it's a business thing he does with all his clients."

Dismissing any other thoughts, she climbed the stairs and went back to her aunt's room.

John Shaw was also thinking about Susanna and wondering if she were shy or just cold. "She really is making any contact difficult. I wonder why she's so defensive and cold. Well, I'll have to bring down those defenses," he decided, "and I will start by getting her to go to lunch with me. Until tomorrow, Susanna!"

Quincy, who normally followed his mistress everywhere, stayed upstairs curled up on the rug. Seeing him as soon as she came into the room, Susanna admired his beauty, his sleekness and grace. But it was his unconditional love that was so wonderful. He really asked for very little in return. As these thoughts passed through her mind, her eyes returned to the letter, now on the seat of the rocker where she had left it. She sat down and began to read it again.

"Quincy, Grandfather Smith has me intrigued. Aunt Susanna must have felt the same way when she read this letter. There are a lot of letters here. This is going to take a while. Maybe we should have another cup of tea and, more important, a Krispy Kreme doughnut. What do you think?"

Quincy, by his reaction, would have people believing he understood every word Susanna spoke. He quickly got up and beat a path to the kitchen and the Krispy Kreme doughnut box they had picked up earlier in the day. He sat by the counter and waited for Susanna to meet him there. When she did get to the kitchen, he used his most imploring look until Susanna gave in and broke up the glazed goody in small pieces for him. Tea brewed and doughnut in hand, she and Quincy returned to Aunt Susanna's bedroom and the letters.

Susanna picked up the wooden box, lifted the letters out, and laid them on the top of the trunk. Carefully opening the cheesecloth material, she took out the first letter. While yellow with age, the letter was in really remarkable condition. It was dated May 4, 1775, and had been written by Abigail Adams to her husband, John. It was written from Braintree, a neighboring town of Weymouth, where Abigail and John Adams made their home. Susanna started to read the letter and thus her long journey into the past began.

Braintree May 4, 1775

I have but little news to write you. Every thing of that kind you will learn by a more accurate hand than mine: things remain much in the same situation here that they were when you went away, there has been no Desent upon the sea coast. Guards are regularly kept, and people seem more settled, and are returning to their husbandry. — I feel somewhat lonesome. Mr. Thaxter is gone home. Mr. Rice is going into the Army as captain of a company. We have no School. I know not what to do with John. — As Government is assumed I suppose Courts of Justice will be established, and in that case there may be Buisness [business] to do. If so would it not be best for Mr. Thaxter to return? They seem to be discouraged in the study of Law, and think there never will be any buisness for them. I could have wishd they had consulted you upon the subject before you went away. Mr. Rice has asked my advice? I tell him I would have him act his pleasure. I dont chuse to advise him either way. — I suppose you will receive 2 or 3 Vol. of that forlorn Wretches [sic] Hutchisons Letters. Among many other things I hear he wrote in 1772 that Deacon Phillips and you had like to have been chosen into the Counsel, but if you had you should have shared the same fate with Bowers. May the fate of Mordeca be his. — There is no body admitted into Town yet. I have made two or 3 attempts to get somebody in, but cannot succeed, so have not been able to do the Buisness you left in charge with me. — I want very much to hear from you, how you stood your journey, and in what state you find yourself now. I felt very anxious about you tho I endeavourd to be very insensible and heroick, yet my heart felt like a heart of Led. The same Night you left me I heard of Mr. Quincy's Death, which at this time was a most melancholy Event, especially as he wrote in minets which he left behind that he had matters of concequence intrusted with him, which for a want of a confident must die with him. — I went to see *his distressed widdow last Saturday at the Coll. and in the afternoon from an allarm they had, she and her sister, with three others of the family took refuge with me, and tarried all night. She desired me to present her regards to you, and let you know she wished you every blessing, should always esteem you as a sincere Friend of her deceased husband. Poor afflicted woman, my heart was wounded for her.—I must quite [quit] the subject, and intreet you to write me by every opportunity. Your Mother desires to be remembered to you. She is with me now. The children send Duty, and their Mamma unfeigned Love.* (3)

Yours,   *Portia*

Wow, what a letter! But, what does all this mean, thought Susanna. Who is Mr. Thaxter? Mr. Rice? And who are Mr. Quincy, Hutchinson and Phillips? What is she referring to about not being admitted to town? How did Mr. Quincy die and what matters of consequence was he referring to? Why did she sign the letter "Portia"?

"Quincy, all these questions must be answered before I can continue. I need to find out as much about Abigail Adams and this particular time in her life to make any sense of these letters. Let's go downstairs and see if Aunt Susanna has any books that can help."

It proved to be a long night for Susanna and Quincy and by the time they had their answers, it was four in the morning. Pouring through Aunt Susanna's collection of books on Abigail and John Adams helped lend insight into the first letter and, more important, a desire to read the rest. Sitting in this old parlor, the years seemed to fade away. Susanna could almost imagine Abigail Adams writing this letter. This old house, she learned, was very similar to the Braintree Farm House of John and Abigail, and a sense of *déjà vu* filled Susanna.

Talking to a dog might not be ideal, but Susanna had a need to vocalize what she had learned and Quincy was the only one available to listen. Fortunately for Susanna, Quincy's best trait was that he was a good listener.

"What an extraordinary woman. To think she never had a formal education. Imagine if her mother had allowed her to go to school how much more she might have achieved! With John Adams gone for so many years helping with the creation of a new nation, so much of the responsibility fell on her shoulders—the running of the farm, the raising of five children, and being a supportive wife. The times were difficult, pre-Revolutionary in fact. So much intrigue and uncertainty. She must have been very lonely!"(4)

Picking up the old letter again, Susanna thought about the people mentioned in it. She felt she had a grip on who they all were and tried to think through the set of events leading up to May 4, 1775. Reading through Aunt Susanna's books gave her an understanding of all of this. For the first time in her life she realized how important her lineage was. The impact of it all astonished her.

"Wow, I'm related to this great lady! Quincy, can you imagine that? I've known this my whole life and never realized how important it is. What's wrong with me?"

Imagining what it must have been like for Abigail Adams during this time suddenly was the most important thing to Susanna. She wanted to feel and know everything.

Looking through the books again, Susanna knew that barely a month before Abigail Adams wrote this letter, the first battle of the Revolutionary War had taken place at Lexington and Concord. On April 19, 1775, British soldiers were marching from Boston. Their plan was to take custody of a large quantity of arms.

As they advanced to Lexington Green, they were met by a local force of "minuteman" who were local militia that were prepared to fight at a minute's notice, as they had been warned by Paul Revere that the British were coming. The same happened in Concord and on back to Boston. The casualties inflicted on the British by these untrained farmers were astounding. The impact of these skirmishes only cemented the cause of the colonists and further reinforced the growth of independence. (5)

"Quincy, let's put the pieces together. Let's think this through all the way. The first battles of the American Revolution at Lexington and Concord occurred three weeks before this letter was written. Think about how horrible it must have been for her. John was away, the British were everywhere, and families were in turmoil. The uncertainty, the fears for her family and the knowledge that everything was changing must have been a heavy burden. Her concerns over her cousin, John Thaxter, and the tutor, Mr. Rice, who were planning on leaving to help in the cause of independence, are very evident.

"No wonder she was upset. The economic loss, if both men left John's law office, would only add to the burden. How would she carry on the business in John's absence? If these two men left, how would they earn an income?

"I wonder what business John left for her to do in Boston. Surely it had to do with the running of the farm. The British control of Boston made it impossible for her to travel in and out of that city. This must have been so frustrating. The fear that John Quincy, her son, would be without formal education or tutoring was another issue. With Mr. Rice and Mr. Thaxter leaving, there would be no school and definitely no tutors. The reference to 1772 and the ill-fated wretch of a governor, Hutchinson, I will have to look up at the library. The papers that were discovered had something to do with John and Deacon Phillips, an associate of John's. I guess I'll find out about the fate of Bowers at the same time.

"What really piques my interest is the death of Josiah Quincy Jr. What did he die from? What information couldn't he divulge? Perhaps the information is in a future letter."

Quincy's loud snoring startled Susanna from these musings. Looking at her watch, she realized that John and the auctioneer would arrive in less than five hours.

"Quincy, I better get some sleep, or I won't be able to get through the day. I'll look at the next letter later today to see if any of this is clearer. In the meantime, I need to go to bed."

Chapter 6

At precisely ten o'clock, John and Jerry Carter were knocking at the door. Jerry Carter was thirty-three, a year younger than John Shaw, but he looked much older. He was heavier than John, and looked like an unmade bed. His shirt was hanging out in the back, his shoelace on his left sneaker was untied and he appeared to have a two-day growth of beard. He was the complete opposite of John, who looked like he just stepped from the pages of *GQ*—they were the personification of *The Odd Couple*. Yet, they were good friends, almost like brothers. When Susanna opened the door they were laughing so hard they couldn't even speak.

"Good morning. Am I interrupting something?'

"We're sorry. Jerry and I were just reminiscing about an incident that happened in our fraternity when we were in college."

"Can you let me in on the joke?"

"I'm afraid this one is x-rated and must be kept a secret. Susanna Smith, meet Jerry Carter, auctioneer extraordinaire."

"Mr. Carter, a pleasure to meet you. Please, both of you, come in."

"What a beautiful home," commented Jerry.

"Thank you, many of the pieces are old and were inherited from past generations. My aunt was the family's historian and took great care of everything that was passed down to her."

"Will everything be auctioned off?"

"I'm not sure. I may want to keep some things. I really haven't had much time to go through all the articles and decide what I want to keep or sell. Right now, I just want to get an estimate to see what value they may have."

"I can do that. Let me go from room to room to get an idea of what's here. Why don't you and John talk about the sale of the house, and when I'm done I'll let you know what I think."

"Would either of you like some coffee?"

"None for me," said Jerry.

"I'll have a cup, Susanna. We can go over my appraisal at the same time."

Sitting at the table in the kitchen, Susanna wondered if everything was moving too fast. Maybe she should slow things down.

Quincy, up to this point, had been held by the collar and had had enough. With the move into the kitchen, he almost wiggled out of his skin in an attempt to be petted by John. John reciprocated and bent down to pet Quincy's ears and head. Comforted, Quincy laid down on the floor next to him.

"Susanna, this old house is in good condition, plus it has historical value. The amount of money you can gain from the sale will depend upon how quickly you want to sell. I place the value somewhere between six-hundred and seven-hundred thousand dollars. If you want to sell quickly, I suggest you put it on the market for five-eighty-five. Frankly, I would advise you to take your time and try to get the full value. You could lose a lot of money if you don't."

"Did you say seven-hundred thousand dollars? That much! For this little house? Surely, you're joking!"

"No, I'm not. We might even be able to get more. You have to understand, just the historical value alone will entice a certain type of buyer."

"I really don't know what to say. I didn't expect it to be worth so much. Do you mind if I take another day to think about this? Aunt Susanna certainly had more assets than I was aware of."

"Please take your time. Don't misunderstand me. I would love to sell this house, but only if you want to. Now how about that lunch!"

Before Susanna could answer, a very excited Jerry Carter came into the kitchen. Looking like the proverbial cat that swallowed the canary, he sat down at the table.

"Susanna, there are many items that would sell well at auction. I'm going to draw up an estimate for an estate sale. We can then sell everything, lock, stock, and barrel. I noticed some letters in the bedroom upstairs. I'd like to buy them for myself. I collect old letters. I can give you a good price. Maybe we can come to some arrangement?"

"I don't think so. Those letters are part of my family history. Draw up your estimate and, in the meantime, I will go through the house and let you know what I'll be taking with me."

"Are you sure we can't come to some arrangement on the letters now?

"No, I'm definitely keeping them."

"Very well, I'll be in touch. I'll call you tomorrow or the next day. John, do you want to have lunch?"

"No thanks, Jerry. I promised Susanna I would take her to lunch today. Some other time."

"Okay, see ya!"

Jerry Carter left Susanna and John sitting at the table. As he walked out the door, he was trying to figure out how he was going to get his hands on those letters.

"Susanna Smith doesn't know what she has. I must get those letters. I could triple my money on the collector's black market," he thought out loud. With that, he got into his car and drove away.

"Susanna, I won't take no for an answer," said John. Let's go. I know you will like this restaurant."

"Quincy has to come with us. We'll take two cars. He can stay in mine. This way, when we're finished you can go on your way without having to bring me back home. If we have enough time after lunch, I might go to the library anyway."

"Okay, just follow me."

Chapter 7

The restaurant was located within a charming inn, the Ivy Cottage. It was a lovely, New England style inn, a larger version of a bed-and-breakfast with a small restaurant. As they drove up, it looked like a Thomas Kinkade painting that had come to life. The inn, true to its name, was covered in ivy. It sat next to a small creek with a waterwheel no longer in operation. The wheel was part of an old mill, which also had long ago ceased working. The outside was pretty with the flowers of May. Iris, pansies and bleeding heart abounded, and there was a fragrance of lilac in the air. Stepping from her car, Susanna was delighted with this beautiful picture.

"John, if the food is as good as this inn looks, for sure I will list Aunt Susanna's house with you."

"I can guarantee it's good. Wait till you see the inside."

The inside of the restaurant was as warm and inviting as the exterior. The small room had tables with crisp, white linen tablecloths. On top of the tables were glass vases with fresh cut spring flowers. A fireplace was at one end and, even though it was May, it was lit and inviting. Antique pieces were placed strategically throughout the small room.

John and Susanna were seated at a table in the corner near the fireplace. As it was early, the restaurant was not crowded. It was a relaxing ambience, a room that one would not want to leave too quickly.

"John, this is lovely! I had no idea that there was a place like this so close to Weymouth."

"It was your aunt who introduced me to this inn. She said it was a true New England experience. I was visiting my father one summer and she suggested we have lunch here. I consider this one of my favorite places because of her."

"There is so much about my aunt I don't know. I'm finding out how many lives she really touched."

The waitress came over to the table and took their order, clam chowder for the two of them, lobster salad for Susanna and crab cakes for John.

"I think you'll really like the chowder. So, you live in New Jersey. What exactly do you do there?"

"I'm the director of financial aid at a small, independent, private college. It is a difficult job, but it can be very rewarding. I help students and parents find a way to finance a college education. Sometimes, I wonder why I do what I do, but then, out of the blue, a graduating student who was once really difficult will come back to me and thank me for my help.

"I have to deal with students, parents, college administrators, the federal government and the state agencies. It gets to be a juggling act sometimes. I have a great staff, and there are many wonderful people at the college who help make the job what it is. How about you? Have you always wanted to sell real estate?"

"I went to Boston University and had planned on going to law school like my father and grandfather before me. Halfway through college, I discovered I wanted to do something, actually anything, other than practice law. I really didn't like it. I liked working with my hands, building things. In my spare time I do carpentry work and help to restore old homes. I did it for a couple of years after I graduated and then decided to get my real estate license. I worked for another broker for a while, then opened my own firm four years ago. I really like what I do, and it gives me the money and the time to indulge in my restoration work and my love of historical things."

"My father was a history professor at the college where I work. He and my Aunt Susanna both shared a passion for history that they must have inherited from my grandfather. I remember sitting in on one of my father's classes and being surprised at how excited he got about his subject. The students loved him. Coming back here to Weymouth and Aunt Susanna's house only reminds me of how much I miss him and my mother."

"I'm so sorry. Your aunt told me what happened. You must have been devastated."

"I was, but Aunt Susanna wouldn't let me dwell on the sadness. She really came to my rescue and made me go on. I will always love her for that."

Before John could answer, the waitress brought their food. The remainder of the meal was passed in an easy silence and enjoyment of good food. When coffee and dessert were served, the need to talk returned.

"John, since you like history so much, I will have to share some very old letters with you. They have been handed down in my family and Aunt Susanna has left them to me. I don't know if you're aware of my relationship to Abigail Adams?"

"Your aunt mentioned it a long time ago, but I really never thought much about it."

I need to go through the letters, but I will be happy to show them to you when I'm done reading. This wonderful lady fascinates me. She was truly an example to be followed. To tell you the truth, I think I would have a hard time living up to her standards. Well, I'm sorry to say this John, but I must get going. Quincy has been in the car for over two hours and I need to get to the library to do some research."

"This has been great. Please allow me to take you here again sometime."

Susanna and John left the restaurant and made their way to the parking lot. Quincy was sleeping on the front seat of the Durango, but was quickly alert when he heard the door locks.

"Thanks again John, I really enjoyed the lunch."

"My pleasure! Please take your time in making a decision about the house. Don't feel rushed. I think your Aunt Susanna would be pleased with your being here and staying at the house. Call me when you make up your mind."

"I'll be sure to do that. I'll call you soon."

Chapter 8

After leaving the restaurant, Susanna took Quincy for a long walk at a nearby park. As she was walking, she thought about lunch, and how she may have misjudged John Shaw. Her first impression was that of a spoiled young man who had had every material thing he ever wanted. Instead, she now realized that he had rebelled against all that affluence, and was really a down-to-earth person. She liked the fact that he worked with his hands and also that he loved history. "There's more to him than what's on the surface," she mused.

"Quincy, let's get going. I want to get to the library and find out the answers to my questions about the letter."

Susanna pulled in front of the library and parked in the lot next to it. This was Aunt Susanna's library. This is where she spent almost forty years of her life. The building's architecture was similar to all the libraries that were built in the early nineteen-twenties. It looked like a much smaller-scaled New York Public Library, without the lions.

Going inside she remembered a time when she was about ten years old and came to visit her aunt at work. The day had been magical. Aunt Susanna made all the books she read come alive. The library was the same, perhaps more automated, but still the same. Susanna felt like she had come home.

Behind the desk was a young woman of about twenty-eight. She had chestnut colored hair and white, flawless skin. There was something vaguely familiar about her. Susanna just couldn't put her finger on it. The nameplate said her name was Mary Connors, and that she was the head librarian.

"Excuse me. I wonder if I can ask you where you keep your historical reference books? I'm looking for material on John and Abigail Adams."

"No problem. I'm not very busy right now. Let me show you where they are."

"Have you been the librarian long? My Aunt Susanna used to be the librarian here."

"You're related to Susanna Smith?"

"Yes. She was my aunt. I've come up to Weymouth to settle her estate."

"Your aunt was a wonderful person. It's because of her that I became a librarian. She taught me everything I know. When she died, I thought I would never get over it, she meant that much to me."

"Thank you for your kind words."

"Now, what can I do to help you? It would really give me a great deal of pleasure to give back a little of the kindness your aunt gave to me."

"I'm doing research on John and Abigail Adams, primarily the year 1775 and perhaps earlier. I'm looking at pre-Revolutionary times especially."

"Well, this section we're in will give you a lot of that information. There are several books on John and Abigail Adams. They were prolific writers. Do you need help, or do you want to do this on your own?"

"I think I'll be fine, but if I run into trouble, I'll give you a yell. Thank you for your time."

"Okay, I'll be at the front desk. I'll check on you later. We close at five o'clock, so you only have about two and a half-hours today, but you certainly can come back tomorrow. We open at nine in the morning."

After Mary Connors left, Susanna got busy. Susanna pulled several books down from the shelf and began to read the life and history of her forebear, Abigail Smith Adams.

Abigail Smith was born on November 22, 1744, in Weymouth, Massachusetts. Her family was well respected in the community. Her father was a Harvard graduate, and was the son of a wealthy merchant. At the time of Abigail's birth, he was a minister in the town of Weymouth. Her mother also came from a wealthy, well-educated family of prominent New Englanders. (6)

Abigail had two sisters and one brother and for all intents and purposes had a happy childhood. Financially, the family was secure and they did not want for anything materially. Shy and quiet, Abigail was sickly as a child. Her parents worried that some disease would end her life at a tender age. Unlike today with the availability of modern drugs, many children died. In fact, Abigail complained that her mother was over-protective and smothering at times. While demanding, her mother taught her the values and morals that she would need to carry her through her turbulent lifetime. (7)

Abigail Adams lacked a formal education. She was taught basic subjects, such as reading and arithmetic. These fundamentals enabled not only Abigail but also many women of the day to carry on basic homemaking duties. Abigail and her sisters were fortunate that their father loved to read and encouraged his daughters to share this same passion. Her father's library was well-stocked and although she lacked a formal education, Abigail became self-taught and one of the most educated women of her time. (8)

The lack of formal education haunted Abigail Adams her entire life. This is evident in the letters she wrote during her lifetime. Her spelling was erratic, her grammar was poor, and even her penmanship bothered her. Yet, without these letters and diaries, a richness and intimate portrait of the eighteenth and nineteenth centuries would be lost forever. Women of later centuries owe a great deal to this strong woman who took an unusual, independent stance on her education. (9)

John and Abigail Adams first met at her sister Mary's wedding. John was ten years older than Abigail and in truth was not taken with her. After the wedding, they did not see each other for another two years. When they did meet the second time, Abigail was older, and something clicked. The chemistry was strong, with a love discovered that would be so dynamic and so extraordinary that no one could shake their resolve. From this meeting on, their fates were sealed. (10)

On October 25, 1764, John and Abigail married and established their home in the town of Braintree, not very far from Weymouth, Abigail's birthplace. Over the course of the next fourteen years, Abigail would have six pregnancies and five children. A way of life was established early in their marriage: She stayed at home and took care of the farm and the children, and John pursued his career as an attorney. He traveled a circuit that would take him as close as Boston and as far away as Maine. The absences were many and Abigail was very distressed to be parted from her beloved John. (11)

In 1768, they moved to Boston, a bustling, and exciting town. This move allowed Abigail to socialize with affluent people, read many newspapers and be present during the early stages of the Revolutionary War. One of the people that Abigail wrote to, and socialized with, was her good friend Mercy Warren, an historian and poet. (12)

In the long periods of separation, Abigail wrote letters to John that were filled with the problems with the farm, their children, extended family, politics, war and other news, and love. This letter writing gave her a way to express her ideas, opinions, and concerns unusual for a woman of her time. Through these letters, a confident, bright, insightful woman emerges. Tough times required strong people and Abigail Adams fit this mold. (13)

The way the letters were addressed, and signed, reflect a side to their marriage that was tender, loving, and at times very sensual. Addressing her letters to "My Dearest Friend" or "Dearest of Friends," Abigail, established a pattern. Not only was her manner of address special, so was her signature. (14)

In February 1775, just prior to Lexington and Concord, Abigail wrote to her dear friend, Mercy Warren, "Is it not better to die the last of British freemen than live the first of British slaves?" Mercy, who was the mother of five sons responded, "Which of us should have the Courage of an Aria or a Portia in a Day of trial like theirs." She was referring to Portia, the wife of Brutus, who was a Roman statesman. Finding this an interesting note from history, from that time on Abigail used the name Portia to sign off on her letters to John. (15)

"Miss Smith. Miss Smith! "

Returning to the present, Susanna was startled to hear her name. She looked up from her books and saw Mary Connors standing next to the table.

"I'm sorry. I was so involved with my reading I didn't hear you at first."

"I just wanted to let you know we will be closing in ten minutes."

"Oh, I've lost track of time! I'll just clean up these books."

"Just put them on the cart and I'll put them away tomorrow."

"Thanks for your help Mary. I'm going to try to come back tomorrow. I still need to look up some more facts. I really haven't touched the meat of the subject yet. I've sort of been reading the *Reader's Digest* version, short and condensed."

"Miss Smith, would you like to go get some coffee or a bite to eat? I would really like to talk to you about your aunt."

"First of all, please call me Susanna. And, yes, let's go for a cup of coffee."

"Great, let me close up and then we can go to the little café down the street—nothing fancy, but the coffee is excellent."

The café was really an updated luncheonette. It was small and clean, and really did have great coffee. After they were served, both of them decided to order a sandwich to go with their steaming beverage.

"Mary, how long did you know my Aunt Susanna?"

"I actually met her while I was in high school. I needed help on a paper I was writing for history class and was told to seek her out. She was really a great historian and knew where to get the information I needed. I liked her immediately. She was warm and caring, almost like a surrogate grandmother. We developed a great relationship through the years. She followed me through college and wrote to me often. When I finished college I came back home and was at a loss as to what I should do with my life. Your aunt suggested I go back to school and get my degree in library science. I took her advice and never looked back. When she retired, she recommended me for the position of town librarian. I got the job, and the rest, as they say, is history. I love what I do and I owe that to your aunt."

"I'm learning a lot about who my aunt was. I'm afraid she was a great aunt, and I was a lousy niece. I hate to admit it, but I took her for granted. I thought she would always be there. She did so much for me, and I did nothing for her in return. I'm meeting so many people she touched during her lifetime. Everyone seems better for knowing her. She changed so many lives."

"Susanna, she talked about you often. She was very proud of you and your achievements. I know for a fact that she never felt you took advantage of her. She loved you very much. Every time she heard from you, she spoke about you with such pride. Please don't feel guilty. I know she wouldn't want that."

"I'm so sorry. I didn't mean to burden you with this. You are really easy to talk to but I feel I'm rambling. Please forgive me."

"Susanna, I know we've just met, but I think we could be friends. We have a lot in common, and I can share some of the memories I have of your aunt. Maybe you can share some of yours. That might help to ease some of your sadness."

"I would like that. I'm trying to settle the estate and decide what to do with everything. When I first got here I thought I would sell the house and the contents, but now I'm beginning to have doubts. There is so much of my family here, and I'm really drawn to the house. There are too many decisions."

"I'll be happy to help you. Tell me what you would like me to do."

"Mary, I don't know what to do myself, but thank you for the offer. I just might take you up on it one of these days.

"I hate to cut this short, but I have to get Quincy home and fed, and then I have to finish up some reading. I will come by the library tomorrow and do some more research. Let's have dinner tomorrow night and we can continue our conversation."

"Quincy is really beautiful. How old is he?"

"He's five years old and still a big baby. He is one of the loves of my life, I don't know what I would do without him. He really is a great companion. So, how does dinner tomorrow sound?"

"Sounds good! See you tomorrow."

Susanna made a few stops on the way back to the house and then walked Quincy. As she pulled into the driveway, she discovered Jerry Carter sitting there in his car.

Seeing her, Jerry opened his door and got out.

"Hi Susanna, hope I didn't startle you."

"I'm a little surprised to see you so soon. I hope you haven't been waiting too long."

"Actually, I have only been here about ten minutes. I completed the estimate on the inventory and brought along a contract for you. I know you are short on time and tried to expedite the process." His sharp tone caused Susanna to look at him as if for the first time.

"Thank you Jerry, if you just leave the paperwork with me I will look it over and give you a call."

"I'm not trying to rush you, but it will take time to get this all set up and you are only going to be up here for a little more than a week. I want you to go home with peace of mind."

"Jerry, I promise I will call you as soon as I read these papers and make a decision."

Susanna hoped this would end the discussion and that he would leave. For some reason, he was making her feel very uncomfortable and she wanted him gone.

She started to open the door of the car and let Quincy out. As she did, Jerry reached out and touched her shoulder. Quincy, acting on instinct, went crazy, barking and growling. He sensed a problem and was protecting his mistress. Jerry responded by jumping back.

"I didn't realize he was so vicious," he said nervously.

"He's not! He just doesn't like anybody touching me—I don't like it either."

"I'm sorry. I didn't mean anything by it"

"Jerry, I have a lot to do. As I've told you twice, I will call you! Goodbye."

Jerry hesitated but decided to retreat and headed back to his car. As he opened the door, he turned and gave Quincy a glaring look, which changed almost immediately when he realized Susanna was looking at him.

"Have a good night. I'll talk to you soon."

With that, he got into his car and drove away.

Susanna watched him pull away and felt uneasy. She opened the door and calmed Quincy down.

"Easy boy. I agree with you. There is something strange about him. I don't trust him either. I really didn't see this undercurrent before. What I don't understand is how John can be such good friends with him. I'll have to ask John about him tomorrow. And furthermore, I didn't like the way he looked at you. I think we should both be careful. Come on, let's get you fed and walked, I have a busy night ahead of me."

Chapter 9

24 May Braintree 1775

Dear One,

Suppose you have had a formidable account of the alarm we had last Sunday morning. When I rose about six oclock I was told that the Drums had been some time beating and that 3 allarm Guns were fired, that Weymouth Bell had been ringing, and Mr. Welds was then ringing. I immediately sent of [off] an express to know the occasion, and found the whole Town in confusion. 3 Sloops and one cutter had come out, and droped anchor just below Great Hill. It was difficult to tell their design, some supposed they were comeing to Germantown others to Weymouth. People women children from the Iron Works flocking down this Way—very woman and child above or from below my Fathers. My Fathers family flying, the Drs. in great distress, as you may well immagine for my Aunt had her

Bed thrown into a cart, into which she got herself, and ordered the boy to drive her of to Bridgewater which he did. The report was to them, that 300 hundred had landed, and were upon their march into Town. The allarm flew [like] lightning, and men from all parts came flocking down till 2000 were collected—but it seems their expidition was to Grape Island for Levet's hay. There it was impossible to reach them for want of Boats, but the sight of so many persons, and the fireing at them prevented their getting more than 3 ton of Hay, tho they had carted much more down to the water. At last they musterd a Lighter, and a Sloop from Hingham which had six port holes. Our men eagerly jumpt on board, and put of for the Island. As soon as they perceived it, they decamped. Our people landed upon [the] Island, and in an instant set fire to the Hay which with the Barn was soon consumed, about 80 ton tis said. We expect soon to be in continual alarms, till something decisive takes place. We wait with longing Expectation in hopes to hear the best accounts from you with regard to union and harmony [etc]. We rejoice greatly on the Arival of Doctor Franklin, as he must certainly be able to inform you very perticuliarly of the situation of affairs in England. I wish you would [write] if you can get time; be as perticuliar as you may, when you write—every one here abouts come[s] to me to hear what accounts I have. I was so unlucky as not to get the Letter you wrote at New York. Capn Beals forgot it, and left it behind. We have a flying report here with regard to New York, but cannot give any credit to, as yet, that they had been engaged with the Ships which Gage sent there and taken them with great looss upon both sides Yesterday we have an account of 3 Ships comeing in to Boston. I believe it is true, as there was a Salute from the other Ships, tho I have not been able to learn from whence they come. Suppose you have had an account of the fire which did much damage to the Warehouses, and added greatly to the distresses of the inhabitants whilst it continued. The bad conduct of General Gage was the means of its doing so much damage.

Tis a fine growing Season having lately had a charming rain, which was much wanted as we had none before for a fortnight. Your meadow is almost fit to mow. Issac talks of leaving you, and going into the Army. I believe he will. Mr. Rice has a prospect of an adjutant place in the Army. I believe he will not be a very hardy Soldier. He has been sick of a fever above this week, and has not been out of his chamber. He is upon the recovery now.

Our House has been upon this alarm in the same Scene of confusion that it was upon the first-Soldiers comeing in for lodging, for Breakfast, for Supper, for Drink [etc. etc]. Sometimes refugees from Boston tierd and fatigued, seek an assilum for a Day or Night, a week—you can hardly imagine how we live.

> "Yet to the Houseless child of want
> our doors are open still
> And tho our portions are but scant
> We give them with good will."

I want to know how you do? How are your Eyes? Is not the weather very hot where you are? The children are well and send Duty to Pappa. This day Month you set

Dear John

of. I have never once inquired when you think it possible to return; as I think you could not give me any satisfactory answer. I have according to your direction wrote to Mr. Dilly, and given it to the care of Capn. Beals who will deliver it with his own hand; I got Mr. Thaxter to take a coppy for me, as I had not time amidst our confusions; I send it to you for your approbation. You will be careful of it as I have no other coppy. My best wishes attend you both for your Health and happiness, and that you may be directed into the wisest and best measures for our Safety, and the Security of our posterity. I wish you was nearer to us. We know not what a day will bring forth, nor what distress one hour may throw us into. Heitherto I have been able to maintain a calmness and presence of Mind, and hope I shall, let the Exigency of the time be what they will.

Mrs. W[arre]n desires to be rememberd to you with her sincere regards. Mr. C[ranc]h and family send their Love. The poor man has a fit of his old disorder. I have not heard one Syllable from Providence since I wrote you last. I wait to hear from you, then shall act accordingly. I dare not discharge any debts with what I have except to Issac, least you should be disappointed of the remainder. Adieu Breakfast calls (16) I also must tell you of Mr. Quincy, there is news about his death since last I set down to write. There is distress about his demise, some feel it was unnatural. [poison] I will send more when I look into it (I)*

your affectionate   Portia

*(I) *Inserted into the original letter. See Chapter Notes*

Susanna finished the letter and heard the telephone ringing.

"Hello."

"Susanna, it's Mary. I wasn't sure if I would see you in the morning. I'm going to be out in the afternoon at a meeting and wanted to make sure we could set up a time for dinner."

"I'm going to try to be at the library around eleven, but we can make plans now. Do you have a favorite place for dinner?"

"There is a place called the Hare and the Tortoise. It's a nice restaurant and the food is good. Have you ever been there?"

"No, I've never eaten there, but I know Aunt Susanna did."

"Your aunt and I had lunch there on occasion, and I think you might like it."

"That would be fine, what time would you like to meet? Would six be okay with you?"

"That would be great! The restaurant is located on Main Street just down from the Court House. It's a favorite of the judges and lawyers. If I don't see you at the library, I will see you there at six. I have some photos I will bring with me. See you then."

"See you tomorrow. Goodnight Mary."

Susanna hung up the telephone and thought about Mary Connors. She liked her and could understand why her Aunt Susanna had. There was sweetness about her, not a cloying sweetness, but an honest kindness and gentleness. But there was also a sharp intelligence that was evident.

Returning to the letters, Susanna reached for the next one and stopped. She had an uneasy feeling and was still unnerved about Jerry Carter's visit. Was she being silly, or was there a hidden motive to his actions? Reading the letters had triggered her memory about how interested Jerry had been in them. Surely he was just looking out for her and was trying to get things started for her. She would at least give him the benefit of the doubt until she talked to John. Still, Susanna was having second thoughts about hiring him.

"Quincy, what do you think? Do you think I'm being silly?"

Alert, Quincy got up from his blanket and sat next to Susanna as if to say, "I'll protect you, don't worry." Susanna automatically rubbed him under his neck and stroked his head.

"You're such a good boy. I love you Quincy, and I'm so glad you're here with me. Well, let me read at least one more of these letters before I go back to the library.

Chapter 10

"John, so glad you could come by. Would you like a drink or something to eat? I'm sure I can find something."

"I'll take a drink, Dad. How about a beer? Do you have any?"

"I think I can find some. Come into the library, I'll be right there."

William Shaw was happy to see his son. He always enjoyed John's company, and was very pleased how fine a young man he turned out to be. They didn't have much opportunity to see each other even though they both lived in Weymouth. Their lives had taken two distinct paths. William would have liked John to follow him in the law and was disappointed when John's interests led him elsewhere. Still, John had turned out to be a hard working, likeable fellow. They shared a wonderful relationship. William was very proud of him.

The library was really an extension of William's law office, beautiful ceiling-to-floor bookcases in mahogany, many first edition books, and comfortable leather chairs in which to sit and read. It was in the high-backed leather chair that John waited for his father to return. Handing him the beer, William thought how much he enjoyed having John in this room.

"How are you making out with Susanna Smith? Has she decided to sell the house?"

"I went over and gave her an appraisal and a sales contract if she wants to list it. I think she is very conflicted. She's a nice woman, but hard to read. I think she is a little insecure and has taken some hard hits in her life. Still I'm not sure what she's going to do. I told her to take her time. I also had Jerry give her an estimate on the contents."

"You did what! I can't understand why you have anything to do with him. He's dishonest and will only use you and make sure that Susanna gets only a small percentage of whatever her possessions are worth."

"Dad, he's changed. I really believe he knows his stuff and will be able to get market value for some of the antiques in the house. If I thought he would do Susanna harm, I never would have suggested him."

"I think you need to at least warn her of his background, and his problems with the law and his clients—not to mention his gambling problem. I'm not happy about this development. I promised her aunt I would look out for her."

"Dad, stop it. Jerry has turned it around. He has stopped drinking, and he has kept his nose clean for over a year. I owe it to him to give him a chance. I promise you this: if I think he's trouble, I'll personally pull him out."

"I have a bad feeling about him, I really don't trust him, but I will defer to your judgment for the moment. Now, let me show you my new book. I found it in an old book store in Boston."

After promising to meet his father for dinner the next night, John left and went home. Watching him leave, William wondered if he should go by the Smith house and see if everything was all right. He felt anxious and didn't trust

Jerry Carter at all. "Maybe I'll go over on Saturday and see if Susanna needs any help," he thought.

"It would be nice to see the house again, to be surrounded by Susanna's things, and memories. Yes, I think I will do that." With that decided, William returned to his chair and his new book.

Chapter 11

Weymouth June [16?] 1775

Dearest One,

I set down to write to you a monday, but really could not compose my-self sufficiently: the anxiety I sufferd from not hearing one syllable from you for more than five weeks; and the new distress ariseing from the arrival of recruits agitated me more than I have been since the never to be forgotten 14 of April.

I have been much revived by receiving two letters from you last Night, one by the servant of your Friend and the other by the Gentlemen you mention, tho they both went to Cambridge, and I have not seen them. I hope to send this as a return to you.

I feard much for your Health when you went away. I must intreat you to be as careful as you can consistant with the Duty you owe your Country. That consideration alone prevaild with me to consent to your departure, in a time so perilous and so hazardous to your family, and with a body so infirm as to require the tenderest care and nursing. I wish you may be supported and divinely assisted in this most important crisis when the fate of empires depend upon your wisdom and conduct. I greatly rejoice to hear of your union, and determination to stand by us.

We cannot but consider the great distance you are from us as a very great misfortune, when our critical situation renders it necessary to hear from you every week, and will be more and more so, as difficulties arise. We now expect our Sea coasts ravaged. Perhaps, the very next Letter I write will inform you that I am driven away from our, yet quiet cottage. Necessity will oblige Gage to take some desperate steps. We are told for Truth, that he is now Eight thousand strong. We live in continual expectation of allarms. Courage I know we have in abundance, conduct I hope we shall not want, but powder—where shall we get a sufficient supply? I wish we may not fail there. Every Town is fill'd with the distressed inhabitants of Boston—our House among others is deserted, and by this time like enough made use of as a Barrack—Mr. Bowdoin with his Lady, are at present in the house of Mrs. Borland, and are a going to Middlebouragh to the house of Judge Oliver. [The] poor Gentlemen is so low, that I apprehend he is hastening to an house not made with Hands—looks like a mere skelliton, speaks faint and low, is racked with a voilent cough, and I think far advanced in a consumption. I went to see him last Saturday. He is very inquisitive of every person with regard to the times, beged I would let him know of the first inteligence I had from you, is very unable to converse by reason of cough. He rides every pleasant Day, and has been kind enough to call at the Door, (tho unable to get out) several times. Says the very name of Hutchinson distresses him. Speaking of him the other day he broke out, "religious Rascal, how I abhor his Name."

Dr. Smythe stopped to see me. He told of Mr. Quincy's last days, felt that there was something amiss. Mr. Quincy had been under durress in the past months and had spoke of secret papers, wich were missing upon his demise. His death was unkind, vomiting, sweats, shortness of breath, wile sickness was present, the Dr. feels he may have been poisnd. A Mr. Page, englishman went by to see him two times before Mr. Quincy's death. Dr Smythe beliefs that he was trying to get the papers, and perhaps did a foul deed. Could he be right? Pray tell me what you think. I will talk with Mrs. Quincy soon and report my findings. [I]*

We have had very dry weather not a rainy day since you left us. The english Grass will not yeald half so great a crop as last year. Fruit promises well, but the Cattepillars have been innumerable.

I wrote you with regard to the money I had got from Providence. I have since that obtain'd the rest. I have done as you directed with regard to the payment of some you mentiond, but it incroachd some upon your Stock. You will write me with regard to what you have necessity for and how I shall convey to you.—Mr. Rice is dissappointed of his place in the Army but has hopes of joining a company

*(I) *See Chapter Notes*

much talked of here under Mr. Hancock when he returns. I came here with some of my cousin Kents who came to see me a day, or two ago, and have left company to write you this afternoon least I should fail of conveyance. Pray be perticuliar when you write as possible— every body wants to hear, and to know what is doing, and what may be communicated, do not fail to inform me. All our Friends desire to be kindly rememberd to you. Gage'es proclamation you will receive by this conveyance. All the records of time cannot produce a blacker page. Satan when driven from the regions of bliss, Exibeted not more malice. Surely the father of lies is superceded.—

Yet we think it the best proclamation he could have issued.

I shall when ever I can, receive and entertain in the best Manner I am capable the Gentlemen who have so generously proferd their Service in our Army. Government is wanted in the Army, and Else where. We see the want of it more from so large a body being together, than when each individual was imployd in his own domestick circle.—My best regards attend every man you esteem. You will make my complements to Mr. Miflin and Lady. I do not now wonder at the regard the Laidies express for a Soldier—every man who wears a cockade appears of double the importance he used to, and I feel a respect for the lowest Subaltern in the Army.—You tell me you know not when you shall see me. I never trust myself long with the terrors which sometimes intrude themselves upon me.

I hope we shall see each other again and rejoice together in happier Days. The little ones are well, and send Duty to Pappa. Don't fail of letting me hear from you by every opportunity, every line is like a precious Relict of the Saints. Pray dont Expose me by a communication of any of my Letters—a very bad Soar upon the middle finger of my right hand has prevented my writing for 3 weeks. This is the 5 Letter I have wrote you. I hope they have all come to hand.—I have a request to make you. Something like the Barrel of Sand suppose you will think it, but really of much more importance to me. It is that you would send out Mr. Bass and purchase me a bundle of pins and put in your trunk for me. The cry for pins is so great that what we used to Buy for 7.6 are now 20 Shillings and not to be had for that. A bundle contains 6 thousand for which I used to give a Dollor, but if you can procure them for 50[shillings] or 3 pound, pray let me have them. Mr. Welch who carries this to head Quarters waits which prevents my adding more than I am with the tenderest Regard[s] your (17)

Portia

"Quincy, the more I read these letters, the more I admire Abigail Adams. The time in which these letters are written was horrendous, never knowing if the British would take over her farm and having to be ready to move at a moment's notice. The longing for John's return is so evident, and what about the intrigue over the death of Josiah Quincy? At the library tomorrow I will try to get more information and fill in some of the missing pieces. Now, let's go for a walk."

Chapter 12

Susanna awoke to a beautiful sunshine filled Friday morning. As she got out of bed, she remembered it was the start of Memorial Day weekend. The tourist season in Massachusetts, and especially Cape Cod, would begin in earnest. She also remembered that she had only one more week to get things settled.

Planning her day over coffee, Susanna decided to go to the library in the morning and finish her own inventory of the contents of the house in the afternoon. She was to meet Mary for dinner at six and was looking forward to it. She really enjoyed Mary's company and would be able to hear more about her aunt. Susanna also wanted to talk to John in person about her encounter with Jerry Carter and decided to stop by John's office after the library.

"A busy day, Quincy. I hope you're up to it. Let's get ready to go."

The trip to the library was uneventful, and Susanna was happy to see Mary at the desk.

"Hi Mary, how are you today?"

"Susanna, good morning. I'm glad you got here before I had to leave for my meeting. Let me help you get started."

"Thanks. I think I'll only be here for a couple of hours. I'm really looking forward to meeting you for dinner tonight."

"So am I. I don't think my meeting will run late, but if it does, don't worry, I'll be there. I made a reservation for six o'clock, so there won't be a problem. I have some pictures ready for you to see and I can't wait for you to taste the food—it really is fabulous. I'll leave you alone, now, so you can get on with your research. I've already pulled out some books for you and left them on the table. If you need anything else, Annie can help you while I'm gone. See you tonight."

With that, Mary left Susanna to her task. Sitting at the table, Susanna picked up the first book *Dearest Friend* by the author Lynne Withey, and began to read.

After Lexington and Concord, American militiamen laid siege to Boston. Camped in the neighboring towns of Charleston, Cambridge and Roxbury, they kept the redcoats bottled up on the peninsula. The British retaliated by closing off the city and prohibiting anyone from entering or leaving. Abigail tried to sneak someone into town to take care of some business matters for John, but he failed in the attempt. Later, a few people were allowed to leave each day, but they could take very few of their possessions with them. According to Abigail, the rules about what they could take out changed daily. British officials drew up a blacklist of men involved in the Tea Party and would not allow them to leave, although Benjamin Edes, printer of the radical Boston Gazette, *managed to escape to Braintree.*

Braintree was not actually threatened at the moment, but no one's life was quite the same. Refugees from Boston needed a place to go, and residents of outlying towns took in friends and relatives. Abigail housed as many people as she could. Some stayed overnight on their way to other destinations. Some stayed a week, some longer. She often provided meals for soldiers, too. The house, she reported to John, was a "Scene of Confusion…you can hardly imagine how we live." One night she housed an entire company of militia on their way to join the encampments outside Boston.

Some of the soldiers slept in the attic and the rest in the barn. The next morning they drilled in the field behind the house, with Johnny proudly marching up and down in their midst.

British troops periodically raided offshore islands for food and hay to feed their horses, adding to everyone's fears of an imminent attack. The redcoats could not move west out of Boston without tangling with American troops, so it seemed logical that they might move out by sea to coastal towns like Weymouth and Braintree. The local militia stepped up their drills and posted regular guards.

In the back of everyone's minds was the realization that they might have to pull up stakes and flee at any moment in the event of an actual attack. Eunice Paine, now living some miles south of Braintree in Taunton, wrote of her fears about an invasion there; Mercy Warren urged Abigail to pay one more visit to Plymouth before the war cut them off. Mary Nicholson wanted to visit Braintree, but her family would not let her travel because of fear of attack. Mary also tried to write Eunice but reported that it was harder to send a letter to Taunton than to England. John's brother, who lived in a remote inland section of Braintree, invited Abigail to go there with the children if the coast were attacked. John, meanwhile, urged Abigail to stay calm and not do anything rash. If an attack actually came, she should "fly to the Woods with our Children."

But when the next major battle came, it was not Braintree or Weymouth but Charlestown, just north of Boston, that suffered. Abigail awoke early to the sound of cannon fire on June 17. A haze of smoke from the guns was visible across the horizon. With Johnny, she climbed to the top of Penn's Hill for a better view. From there she could see that Boston—or some place very near it—was under attack, and that this was no mere skirmish like the fighting at Lexington and Concord.

Two days later she still had no clear information about the battle. Only one tragic piece of news was definite: Joseph Warren was dead. The handsome young physician had been one of their most intimate friends and, with John, one of the earliest advocates of American rights. Now he was one of America's first casualties. Abigail reported the news to John with a heavy heart. It had not taken long for the reality of the war to affect them personally.

John was concerned with philosophical unity, with charting the political course of America in broad terms. Abigail lived with the reality of war and slow-moving fleets were not to her liking. "I want you to be more perticuliar," she wrote to John with a touch of asperity. "Does every Member [of Congress] feel for us? Can they realize what we suffer? And can they believe with what patience and fortitude we endure the conflict— nor do we even tremble at the frowns of power." Bostonians were "the most abject slaves under the most cruel and despotick of Tyrants," she reported. Inhabitants were forbidden to leave their homes. They had no fresh vegetables or fish. "A Lady who lived opposite says she saw raw meat cut and hacked upon her Mahagona Tables, and her superb damask curtain and cushings exposed to the rain as if they were of no value." Desperate to escape, some people paid as much as forty dollars for passes out of the city, and it was widely believed that several Americans had been jailed.

Like everyone else, Abigail lived this kind of divided existence. One day she was helping refugees find shelter; another day she was supervising the mowing of hay or trying to keep caterpillars out of the fruit trees. The summer of 1775 was unusually hot and dry, and she worried that the drought would damage the crops. She often concluded letters to John reporting the gravest events with requests that he send her pins or such other scarce necessities as coffee, sugar and pepper.

As always, John's absence was the greatest hardship for her. Her distress at his absence intensified during periods of quiet, when she had leisure to reflect on the happenings around her. John's work left him little time to write long letters, and she knew it. But still, at times she felt neglected. "I have received a good deal of paper from you; I wish it had been more covered," she complained in July. Soon afterwards she told him that not only were his letters too short, but they had no feeling. "I want some sentimental Effusions of the Heart," She wrote. "I am sure you are not *destitute of them or are they all absorbed in the great publick…I lay claim to a Larger share than I have had."*(18)

Susanna looked up from her reading and looked at the clock on the wall. It was now one-thirty and she had much to do in the afternoon. Reluctant to stop, she closed the book. She would not be able to come back on Monday, so Susanna decided to check the book out and read more at home later.

As she went to the front desk, Susanna remembered Mary had a meeting and saw a young lady that must be Annie sitting at the desk.

"Hi, is it possible to check this book out? I'm a visitor, not a resident."

Two of the greenest eyes looked up and stared at Susanna.

"You must be Miss Smith. Miss Connors told me that if you needed to borrow a book to let you go ahead and do it, that she knew where to reach you. Here, let me stamp it and notate who has it. Can I do anything else for you?"

"No thanks, I think I will take only this book for now."

Picking up the book, Susanna headed for the door and the house.

It was a busy afternoon, and Susanna achieved a great deal. As she looked through the house she was amazed at all the beautiful antiques. Her lack of knowledge about the items upset her but she knew they had monetary value and would fetch a good price at auction. Still, was that what she wanted to do, sell them? These things had meant so much to Aunt Susanna. How could she justify these items going to complete strangers? Yet, what was she going to do with all these things? They would never fit in her home in New Jersey.

"Oh what am I going to do?" said out loud, though she knew no one could answer this question but herself.

Earlier, Susanna had tried to reach John to ask him about Jerry Carter, but his receptionist told her that he had gotten an early start on the holiday weekend. He would be back in the office on Tuesday, so she left her number for him to return the call. Her concerns would just have to wait until then.

Chapter 13

Arriving at the Hare and Tortoise precisely at six o'clock, Susanna was delighted with the ambience of the restaurant and could see why her Aunt Susanna had liked it so much. It was situated near the courthouse, and its décor was reminiscent of an old English Pub, dark wooden benches, high tables, and pictures of hunting scenes, of riding to the hounds, and, not surprisingly, of hares and tortoises. Crisp white linens and fresh flowers in Toby Mugs were on the tables. To the right of the dining room was a bar with booths on one side. There were two dart boards, one on each side of the bar. Two men were already playing, even at this early hour. It appeared to be a Friday night after-work meeting of two good friends.

Susanna walked up to the hostess and told her that she was meeting Mary Connors.

"I don't believe she's here yet. Would you like to be seated, or would you like to wait for her at the bar?"

"I'd like to be seated, thanks. I'll wait for her in the dining room."

"Please, follow me."

Susanna followed the hostess through the dining room. As she was reaching her table, she noticed that John and William Shaw were talking at a table nearby. They noticed her at exactly the same time.

"Miss Smith, how nice to see you again," said William.

"Mr. Shaw! John! What a pleasant surprise, and please, Mr. Shaw, call me Susanna."

"Susanna, are you dining alone? If so please join us," John said with delight.

"Actually, I'm waiting for Mary Connors. We're meeting for dinner tonight. I thought she would be here by now. Wait! Here she comes."

"Susanna, sorry I'm late. Hi, Mr. Shaw, John, I didn't expect to see you here. If I'd have known you were coming here, I would have come with you from the meeting."

"Meeting?"

"Yes. Mr. Shaw and I serve on a committee that will decide how to best use your Aunt's bequest to update the technology in the library."

"Please, won't you both join us? We've only just arrived ourselves and would love to have your company. Here let me help you with the chairs," William said.

The little group got organized quickly and the waiter took their drink order. Susanna and Mary both had wine, John had a Sam Adams beer, and Mr. Shaw a bourbon Old Fashioned. Susanna didn't know why, but she suddenly felt very happy to be here in this restaurant with this group. They felt like old friends and she was very comfortable for the first time since coming to Weymouth.

"Susanna, how did you make out today?" queried Mary.

"Great! I even borrowed a book to finish up some of my research."

"Research? What are you researching?" asked Mr. Shaw.

"I've been doing some work on my family history. Aunt Susanna left me some old letters written by Abigail Adams and I'm trying to find out as much about her as I can. I always knew I was descended from her lineage but it didn't have any impact until I started reading these letters. She was a remarkable woman, someone to be very proud of. There is so much angst and longing in these letters that I had to get to know her better. I've been going to the library and now have some knowledge of the times in which she lived, but I need to know more."

"Your Aunt was quite knowledgeable in this area. We had many long talks about it. Perhaps I can help. I practice law, but my real love is American history, primarily the time of which you speak. I would love to show you my library. Perhaps there are some books that might be of use to you. Better yet, perhaps you would allow me to take you to the Adams National Historic Park in Quincy. The park includes the 17th-century saltbox houses where John Adams and John Quincy Adams were born, and the Old House, where the Adams family and heirs lived from 1788 to 1927. There's also the First United Parish Church where John and Abigail are entombed. Their son, John Quincy, and his wife, Louisa, are entombed there as well. (19) I think you might enjoy this trip back into your family history. Also, we could go to Abigail's birthplace in Weymouth if you like. What do you say? Is it a date?"

"I would really like that. When would you like to go?"

"Would tomorrow be all right? I could pick you up at the house at nine in the morning and we could have the whole day."

"That's great! I'll be ready at nine."

"Would anyone like to join us? I didn't mean to leave anyone out. John? Mary? Are you interested?"

"Dad, thanks but I have an appointment for a house restoration this weekend. I won't be able to do anything until Monday."

"How about you, Mary?"

"Mr. Shaw, I can't. I'm off tomorrow to visit my mom and dad. The library is closed on Monday and I want to take advantage of the long weekend. Since they retired to Martha's Vineyard, I don't get to see them as much I would like to. You and Susanna go and have a wonderful day."

The waiter came over and told the group the specials of the day. Everything sounded so good, it was hard to make a decision. The waiter took their orders and retreated to the kitchen to have them prepared. Once he left, the conversation continued.

"Susanna, I used to come here often with your aunt. This was one of her favorite places, the other was the Ivy Inn. I should take you there sometime."

"I've been there, and I liked it there as well. I can understand why Aunt Susanna liked both places."

Looking at John as she spoke, Susanna couldn't help but notice the look of amusement in William Shaw's eyes. He said nothing in response, but he certainly was aware that there was something stirring between John and Susanna.

"I brought some pictures for you to look at, Susanna," said Mary. "Mr. Shaw, I think you may be in some of these photos. They are of the library picnics and book drive carnivals that Ms. Smith held every year. They served a dual purpose, fund-raising for the library and a consciousness raising to get more people to read books. Your aunt was very successful. Look at this one. I think that young clown is you, John!"

"Let me see that," said John.

The rest of the evening passed with good food, fond memories and promises to meet again. Susanna heard many wonderful stories about her aunt. The sadness that had disappeared after her arrival came back with a vengeance. She found herself upset that she didn't know her aunt like her friends had—almost angry that she missed the opportunity to know that portion of her family life.

"Young ladies this has been delightful. I will let John escort you both to your cars safely. Be careful driving and have a safe journey home. Susanna, I will pick you up at nine. I look forward to our day tomorrow. Goodnight."

John and Susanna walked Mary to her car, which was parked on the street, and watched her get in and drive off. They went to Susanna's car, which she had placed in the restaurant parking lot. Susanna always did this when she had Quincy with her. She liked to feel he was secure when she left him. Quincy heard them coming and his ears perked up and so did he.

"Hi Quincy, how are you boy? Have you been sleeping?" asked John.

Quincy was beside himself. His little stubby tail was wagging out of control. John rubbed his ears and stroked his head. Susanna watched the interplay between them and realized that this was a kind man. As a dog owner and lover of animals, she knew that Quincy was a good judge of character and liked John, too.

"Well, I better let you go. I know you'll have a great day with my Dad tomorrow. You will really like the Adams Homestead. Have a good time. I'll get back up with you on Monday. Goodnight."

John watched Susanna get into her car and waved goodbye. He watched her go down the Main Street and then turn toward home. He thought about how much he liked Susanna Smith and how he wished she would decide not to sell and perhaps make her home in the area. Maybe if she did that he could get to know her better. He would like that. She had a lot of her aunt in her and that was to be admired. Shaking his head, he walked to his car and went home to pack for his weekend away.

Chapter 14

Susanna pulled into the driveway and had a feeling of foreboding. Something was wrong but she couldn't put her finger on it and tried to shake it off. Quincy was acting odd as well. When she opened the car door, Quincy went flying out of the car barking and growling all the way to the front door of the house. He was out of control and so out of character. Susanna ran to the front door and tried to quiet him down. As she got close to the door she realized it wasn't closed properly. Sure she had locked the door before she left, Susanna became alarmed and cautiously opened the door. Quincy went charging in and ran from room to room, smelling and sniffing every inch of space he could. Susanna reached for the light and put it on.

The scream that came from her mouth was more from the horror of what she saw than from fright. The house had been viciously ransacked. Everything was tossed and knocked over. Papers and broken glass were everywhere and in every room. Each room was in the same state. Susanna went upstairs and found the mess there as well. She sat down on the rocker and began to cry.

"Quincy, how could anybody do this? Why destroy everything? Why not just take what you want and leave? I don't understand this. How can anybody be that rotten.

"Maybe I should call John. No, I can't ruin his weekend, and why would he come anyway? No, I better call the police and report this."

Susanna dialed the number and reported the break-in to the police dispatcher.

"Ma'am, is anyone still in the house?"

"No, whoever did this is gone," replied Susanna.

"I will send a patrol car right away. Please don't touch anything."

"Thank you, I'll be careful. I'll also put my dog away in the car before they get here."

Within minutes the police arrived and, shortly after, a detective showed up. Susanna put Quincy in the car to get him out of the way. He hadn't calmed down since they arrived home. She was afraid that the police would get annoyed and felt it was the safest course to take.

"Quincy, I'm sorry, but I think you should stay here for the moment. It will be better for you. I'll come get you when things calm down. I can't imagine what might have happened to you if I had left you home. Oh, Quincy! What would I do without you?"

Detective Maher was looking around the rooms and after a careful search came into the kitchen to talk to Susanna.

"Ms. Smith, the crime scene investigators will be here shortly to look for evidence. In the meantime, do you know anyone who would do this?"

"Detective Maher, I have no idea who did this. I've been here less than a week. I came up here to settle my aunt's estate. I was deciding what to do with the house as well as the contents when this happened."

"From the way the destruction occurred it looks to me like someone had an axe to grind. It almost looks like they were searching for something and didn't find it and decided to wreck the place. Do you know what's missing?" asked Detective Maher.

"I don't know. I really haven't looked yet. Fortunately, I just made a list of what's in the house. Can I go through the list and let you know?"

"Do you want me to take you somewhere? Or do you have a friend you can stay with?" he asked with concern.

"No, I would like to stay here," Susanna said.

"It might be better if you didn't. Whoever did this, if they didn't find what they wanted, might come back. Please think about it."

"No, I have Quincy."

"Quincy?"

"He's my dog," said Susanna.

"That must be the beautiful dog in the Durango outside. What type of dog is it?"

"He's a Weimaraner. It's a German breed. They were originally bred for the hunting of big game. They're known for their friendliness, and their fearlessness. He's a good watchdog and will keep me safe. I feel secure with him. I'll be all right. I need to stay and put things right. I can't leave the place looking like this."

"The crime scene investigators are here. Let me tell them what I'm looking for. I'll be right back."

Susanna looked at the front door and saw two men arrive with cases in hand. The cases looked like toolboxes and contained equipment necessary for them to do their job. After conferring with Detective Maher, the investigators went to work.

Returning to Susanna, Detective Maher continued the conversation.

"Well, I'll have a squad car go by every hour. If you need anything, let them know. I'll also need you to come to the station tomorrow and fill out a report. The crime scene investigators will need another couple of hours to finish and then you'll be able to clean up."

"Thanks Detective Maher. I appreciate your help. You've been very kind."

By three o'clock in the morning everyone was gone and Quincy was freed from his confinement and back in the house. The place looked like a hurricane had blown through it. Susanna went into the parlor and began to pick up the pictures that had been tossed on the floor from the piano. Many of the frames were broken and the glass was shattered but fortunately the pictures themselves were still intact. The frames could be replaced, and Susanna suddenly felt very relieved that the pictures were okay.

"Why did this happen?" She wondered.

Quincy came over and sat down next to Susanna. He was still a little agitated, but had calmed down. Susanna rubbed his neck and soothed him.

"Its all right boy, we can put this all back together. I agree, I don't like it and I'm upset too. It's a good thing I put the letters back in their box and put them in the car. They might have been stolen. I'm so glad I listened to my inner voice."

With that said, Susanna thought about Jerry Carter and his desire for the letters. Could it be possible he did this? Could he have gotten that angry when he didn't find the letters? No, surely he couldn't be that sick.

"I'm just upset and can't think straight. I wonder if I should mention this to Detective Maher? Quincy, let's go out and get the box. I think it's safer in the house now. I should read some of the letters anyway. Let's look for the squad car as well."

Chapter 15

Dearest Friend *Sunday June 18 1775*

The Day; perhaps the decisive Day is come on which the fate of America depends. My bursting Heart must find vent at my pen. I have just heard that our dear Friend Dr. Warren is no more but fell gloriously fighting for his Country saying better to die honourably in the field than ignominiously hang upon the Gallows. Great is our Loss. He has distinguished himself in every engagement, by his courage and fortitude, by animating the Soldiers and leading them on by his own example. A particular account of these dreadful, but I hope Glorious Days will be transmitted you, no doubt in the exactest manner.

The race is not to the swift, nor the battle to the strong, but the God of Israel is he that giveth strength and power unto his people. Trust in him at all times, ye people pour out your hearts before him. God is a refuge for us.—Charlstown is laid in ashes. The Battle began upon our intrenchments upon Bunkers Hill, a Saturday morning about 3 o clock and has not ceased yet and tis now 3 o'clock Sabbeth afternoon.

Tis expected they will come out over the Neck to night, and a dreadful Battle must ensue. Almighty God cover the heads of our Country men, and be a shield to our Dear Friends. How [many ha]ve fallen we know not—the constant roar of the cannon is so [distre]ssing that we can not Eat, Drink or Sleep. May we be supported and sustaind in the dreadful conflict. I shall tarry here till tis thought unsafe by my Friends, and then I have secured myself a retreat at your Brothers who has kindly offered me part of his house. I cannot compose myself to write any further at present. I will add more as I hear further.

Tuesday afternoon [20 June]

I have been so much agitated that I have not been able to write since Sabbeth day. When I say that ten thousand reports are passing vague and uncertain as the wind I believe I speak the Truth. I am not able to give you any authentick account of last Saturday, but you will not be destitute of intelligence. Coll. Palmer has just sent me word that he has an opportunity of conveyance. Incorrect as this scrawl will be, it shall go. I wrote you last Saturday morning. In the afternoon I received your kind favour of the 2 june, and that you sent me by Captn. Beals at the same time.—I ardently pray that you may be supported thro the arduous task you have before you. I wish I could contradict the report of the Doctors Death, but tis a lamentable Truth, and the tears of multitudes pay tribute to his memory. Those favorite lines [of] Collin continually sound in my Ears

Dear John

How sleep the Brave who sink to rest
By all their Countrys wishes blest?
When Spring with dew'ey fingers cold
Returns to deck their Hallowed mould
She their [there] shall dress a sweeter Sod
Than fancys feet has ever trod.
By fairy hands their knell is rung
By forms unseen their Dirge is sung
Their [There] Honour comes a pilgrim grey
To Bless the turf that wraps their Clay
And freedom shall a while repair
To Dwell a weeping Hermit there.

I rejoice in the prospect of the plenty you inform me of, but cannot say we have the same agreeable veiw here. The drought is very severe, and things look but poorly.

Mr. Rice and Thaxter, unkle Quincy, Col. Quincy, Mr. Wibert all desire to be rememberd, so do all our family. Nabby will write by the next conveyance.

I have not seen Mrs. Quincy yet, but will when possible. Please send me your favours soon, I must know what you think. [I]

I must close, as the Deacon w[aits.] I have not pretended to be perticuliar with regard to what I have heard, because I know you will collect better intelligence. The Spirits of the people are very good. The loss of Charlstown affects them no more than a Drop in the Bucket. —I am Most sincerely yours, (20)

Portia

*(I) *See Chapter Notes.*

Susanna picked up another letter and decided to read one more before she called it a night. Mr. Shaw would be there at nine, and that was only five hours away. She would have to cancel their day. Maybe she could catch him before he left his house. Maybe she should ask him to go with her. "I'll ask him in the morning," she decided. "Just one more letter."

Dearest Friend *June 25 1775 Braintree*

My Father has been more affected with the destruction of Charlstown, than with any thing which has heretofore taken place. Why should not his countanance be sad when the city, the place of his Fathers Sepulchers lieth waste, and the gates thereof are consumed with fire, scarcly one stone remaineth upon an other. But in the midst of sorrow we have abundant cause of thankfulness that so few of our Breathren are numberd with the slain, whilst our enimies were cut down like the Grass before the Sythe. But one officer of all the Welch fuzelers remains to tell his story. Many poor wretches dye for want of proper assistance and care of their wounds.

Every account agrees in 14 and 15 hundred slain and wounded upon their side nor can I learn that they dissemble the number themselves. We had some Heroes that day who fought with amazing intrepidity, and courage

"Extremity is the trier of Spirits-
Common chances common men will bear;
And when the Sea is calm all boats alike
Shew mastership in floating, but fortunes blows
When most struck home, being bravely warded, crave
A noble cunning."

Shakespear

Dear John

I hear that General How should say the Battle upon the plains of Abram was but a Bauble to do this. When we consider all the circumstances attending this action we stand astonished that our people were not all cut of. They had but one hundred foot intrenched, the number who were engaged, did not exceed 800, and they [had] not half amunition enough. The reinforcements not able to get to them seasonably, the tide was up and high, so that their floating batteries came upon each side of the causway and their row gallies keeping a continual fire. Added to this fire from fort hill and from the Ship, the Town in flames all round them and the heat from the flames so intence as scarcely to be borne; the day one of the hottest we have had this season and the wind blowing the smoke in their faces—only figure to yourself all these circumstances, and then consider that we do not count 60 Men lost. My Heart overflows at the recollection.

We live in continual Expectation of Hostilities. Scarcely a day that does not produce some, but like Good Nehemiah having made our prayer with God, and set the people with their Swords, their Spears and their bows we will say unto them, Be not affraid of them. Remember the Lord who is great and terrible, and fight for your Breathren, your sons and your daughters, your wives and your houses.

I have just received your of the 17 of june in 7 days only. Every line from that far Country is precious. You do not tell me how you do, but I will hope better.—Alass you little thought what distress we were in the day you wrote. They delight in molesting us upon the Sabbeth. Two Sabbeths we have been in such Alarms that we have had no meeting. This day we have set under our own vine in quietness, have heard Mr. Taft, from psalms. The Lord is good to all and his tender mercies are over all his works. The good man was earnest and pathetick. I could forgive his weakness for the sake of his sincerity—but I long for a Cooper and an Elliot. I want a person who has feeling and sensibility who can take one up with him.

    And in his Duty prompt at every call
    Can watch, and weep, and pray, and feel for all."

Mr. Rice joins General Heaths regiment to morrow as adjutant. Your brother is very desirous of being in the army, but your good Mother is really voilent against it. I cannot persuaid nor reason her into a consent. Neither he nor I dare let her know that he is trying for a place. My Brother has a Captains commission, and is stationd at Cambridge. I thought you had the best of intelligence or I should have taken pains to have been more perticuliar. As to Boston, there are many persons yet there who would be glad to get out if they could. Mr. Boylstone and Mr. Gill the printer with his family are held upon the black list tis said. Tis certain they watch them so narrowly that they cannot escape, nor your Brother Swift and family. Mr. Mather got out a day or two before Charlstown was distroyed, and had lodged his papers and what else he got out at Mr. Carys, but they were all consumed. So were many other peoples, who thought they might trust their little there; till teams could be procured to remove them. The people from the Alms house and work house were sent to the lines last week, to make room for their wounded they say.

Dear John

  Medford people are all removed. Every sea port seems in motion.—O *North!* may the Groans and cryes of the injured and oppressed *Harrow* up thy Soul. We have a prodigious *Army,* but we lack many accomadations which we need. I hope the appointment of these new Generals will give satisfaction. They must be proof against calumny. In a contest like this continual reports are circulated by our *Enimies,* and they catch with the unwary and the gaping croud who are ready to listen to the marvellous, without considering of consequences even tho there best *Friends* are injured.—I have not venturd to inquire one word of you about your return. I do not know whether I ought to wish for it—it seems as if your sitting together was absolutely necessary whilst every day is big with Events.

  Mr. Bowdoin called a fryday and took his leave of me desiring I would present his affectionate regards to you. I have hopes that he will recover—he has mended a good deal. He wished he could have staid in *Braintree,* but his *Lady* was fearful.

  I have often heard that fear makes people loving. I never was so much noticed by some people as I have been since you went out of *Town,* or rather since the 19 of *April. Mr. W[inslo]ws* family are determined to be sociable. *Mr. A——n* are quite *Friendly.*—*Nabby Johny Charly Tommy* all send duty. *Tom* says I wish I could see par. You would laugh to see them all run upon the sight of a *Letter*—like chickens for a crum, when the *Hen* clucks. *Charls* says mar *What* is it any good news? and who is for us and who against us, is the continual inquiry.—Brother and *Sister Cranch* send their *Love.* He has been very well since he removed, for him, and has full employ in his Buisness. Unkel Quincy calls to hear most every day, and as for the Parson, he determines I shall not make the same complaint I did last time, for he comes every other day.

I went to see the Widow Quincy who is still much distressed. I inquired of the night of her beloved husband's death. She informs me that his illness was of a 2 or 3 day time. Quickly he worsened and then passed with much discomfort. She has also talked of Mr. Page's visits. Mr. Quincy was much disturbd after the visits but would not speak of them. When told of Dr. Smythe's thoughts she agreed. Mr. Page is still in Boston and protected by the military there. There must be truth to these thoughts. I long to hear your opinions. [I]*

Tis exceeding dry weather. We have not had any rain for a long time. Bracket has mowed the medow and over the way, but it will not be a last years crop. Pray let me hear from you by every opportunity till I have the joy of once more meeting you. Yours ever more, (21)

Portia

*(I) *See Chapter Notes.*

Chapter 16

Susanna awoke with a start. The doorbell was ringing and Quincy was barking at the noise. Looking at her watch, Susanna realized it was nine o'clock and that she had fallen asleep in the chair reading the letters. It must be Mr. Shaw, she thought, and quickly got up to answer the door.

"Hello, I was beginning to think I'd been stood up."

"I'm so sorry, how long have you been here?"

William Shaw noticed that Susanna was in the same clothes she wore at dinner. She was also very pale and looked upset. He paused and then responded.

"I've been ringing the bell for about five minutes. Are you all right? "

"No, I'm not. I wanted to catch you before you left the house, but I overslept. Please come in and let me tell you what has happened."

"Look at this place! Susanna, who did this?"

"Please, let me get you a chair, and I will explain."

Susanna went through all the activities of the night before, from when she arrived home until the police left her door. She also told Mr. Shaw that she had to call off their plans for the day because she had to go to the police station and give Detective Maher an inventory of what was stolen. Among the missing items was a silver tea set that had been made by the silversmith Paul Revere. This spectacular piece had been Aunt Susanna's pride and joy, and she used it whenever she could. Then she told Mr. Shaw her thoughts and worries about Jerry Carter and asked him if she should mention these to the police.

"I don't want to get anybody in trouble. I have no proof, just an uneasiness and intuition about this. He was very interested in the letters. Also, he was here Thursday night when I got back from the library, and he made me very uncomfortable. Quincy growled and carried on when Jerry touched me on the shoulder, and I was afraid he might attack Jerry. Quincy is a pest, but he's a mild-mannered dog that wouldn't hurt a fly. He had to sense something for him to act that way. Jerry was also very insistent. He seemed troubled and acted very stressed and jittery. I don't know, maybe it's me. Perhaps it's just coming back to Weymouth. I can't explain what I mean very well."

"Susanna, I'm going with you to the police station. I want you to tell Detective Maher what you just told me. I think it's very important you tell him everything. The very fact that you locked up the letters in the car tells me that you suspected something. The wanton destruction of this house indicates that someone was angry and perhaps didn't find what they wanted. They may come back, and this we can't allow to happen. Why didn't you call me right away? You should not have been allowed to stay here last night. I'm going to tell the detective about that and give him an earful!"

"He wanted me to stay somewhere else and I told him I wouldn't go. I wanted to stay here. He had a patrol car go by every hour and made sure I had the telephone at hand at all times. You mustn't blame him."

"You must come and stay with me until we find out who did this. I have a large house and there's plenty of room. I won't take no for an answer."

"I can't, Mr. Shaw. I have Quincy, and, besides, I've only a week to make some sense out of this mess. I have to get a clean-up crew in here to help me. I thought I would be able to do it by myself, but the extent of the damage is too much for me to handle alone."

"We'll talk about this later, young lady. Why don't you freshen up and I'll take you to breakfast. After that we'll go to give your report. I think you should pack up the letters and bring them along with you as well. Go on, I'll wait."

As he waited, William Shaw noticed the photographs that Susanna had picked up and placed back on the piano. He saw Susanna's aunt's photo as a young girl and then he saw his own. He smiled and remembered the times past and wished he could go back. He looked at the room and looked past the mess to the memories that had been made here. Quincy had been watching this activity and especially this man. He had decided Mr. Shaw must be okay, for he came over and placed his head in William Shaw's hand. Startled for a minute, William looked down and laughed.

"Well, what do we have here? Looking for some attention are you? I think you know more than the humans do. I bet you know who did this, don't you? I wish we all had your sense of smell. You really are a beauty. I can see why Susanna loves you so. Come on, let's go to the kitchen and find your food. The least I can do is feed you and give you some fresh water while we're waiting."

Just after Quincy finished eating, the front door bell rang. Susanna had not come down yet, so Mr. Shaw went to the front door to see who was there. Cautiously opening the door, he discovered a short, older woman with grey streaked red hair and a suitcase on the doorstep. She was fair skinned and had piercing blue eyes and an upturned nose. William thought she must have been a beautiful young girl for she was surely an attractive woman now. When the woman opened her mouth, he heard her soft lilting accent. Quincy was excited, as if he knew the woman.

"I'm looking for Susanna Smith, am I at the right address? And if I am, may I ask who you are and what you're doing in her house? Quincy, my good young dog, are you behaving?"

Startled by her frankness, William was speechless. It took him a minute to find his voice, and when he did, he realized that he was on the defensive.

"I'm William Shaw, Susanna's attorney. Who are you?"

Looking past William into the house, she could see the mess and let out a shriek. "I knew it! I had a premonition. I knew there would be trouble. Where's Susanna? Is she all right? I need to see for myself."

"Mrs. O'Hara, what are you doing here? How did you find me? Is everything okay at home?" Susanna said, as she came running down the stairs.

Mrs. O'Hara ran to Susanna and hugged her tight, pulled back a little and looked her up and down to make sure she was really all right.

"Oh Darlin', I am so happy to see you. What happened here? What a mess! I warned you something would happen."

"Calm down, Mrs. O' Hara, I'm fine and so is Quincy. We had a break-in last night and I was just about ready to leave for the police station. Why are you here?"

"I had a dream last night. You were in it and you were in trouble. You were crying and you were running, looking for something—I don't know what—it wasn't clear in the dream. There was a faceless man, as well, who I sensed was trouble. I got up and packed. I left immediately and came right here. I just knew you were in trouble. This proves it. I'm not leaving here unless you come with me," she said, with such determination that William Shaw almost chuckled.

"Susanna, would you please inform Mrs. O'Hara that I'm not a mass murderer and that you're in good hands."

"I'm sorry. Mrs. O'Hara, this is Mr. Shaw. He was my Aunt Susanna's attorney and is now mine. He was going to go to the police station with me."

"Well, I think he would, if he's worth his salt. Why did he let you stay here by yourself? I hope he's a better lawyer than a protector."

"Mrs. O'Hara, please stop it. Mr. Shaw has done everything he can to help and it was my choice to stay here. He didn't even know about this until this morning, so please give him a break."

"I'm sorry, Mr. Shaw, but I'm worried about Susanna," said Mrs. O'Hara.

"Please, I understand. I'm worried about Susanna too! We must go to see the police and give a report. Then we'll see about the house. Would you be able to stay here with Quincy until we get back? The police have a squad car going by every hour and I think you'll be safe for the time we would be gone."

"I think that's a good idea. You two go, I will watch the house and take care of Quincy. These hooligans won't do any more damage with me here. I will also make a nice pot of tea, and if I can find the items I need, some scones for you when you get back. Go on with you now. Time's a wastin'."

Chapter 17

As William and Susanna were leaving for the police station, a man was sitting in his car across town, pondering what to do next. Jerry Carter hadn't slept and, if possible, looked more disheveled than usual. He realized he would most likely be in trouble with the police soon, but this was the lesser of the two evils plaguing him. He was in debt to his bookies for almost $200,000 and with the interest rising his situation was getting worse. He had only twenty-four hours to settle his debt, and he was nowhere near having that kind of money.

His cell phone was ringing and Jerry looked at the caller ID. Deciding whether or not to answer, he finally made up his mind and clicked in.

"Hello!"

"Hey, Jerry, it's Joey. How ya doin'?"

"I'm okay," said Jerry

"Jerry, you're runnin' outta time. Do ya have the money?"

"You'll have the money tomorrow like I said."

"Okay Jerry, it would be a shame to see that pretty face get messed up. Me and the boys will be waitin' for ya tomorrow at one. See ya at Sal's—don't be late!"

"Damn Susanna Smith! Where are those letters? If only she had sold them to me I'd have the money right now. Why weren't they in the house? I only have a day to find them and sell them. Where could she have them? Surely not in a safe deposit box. Maybe they're in her car! I'll have to wait until later and look for her. The problem is that dog, she never goes anywhere without that mutt."

These thoughts were spinning through his mind, and Jerry was getting more agitated as the day wore on. He'd bring the items he had taken from the house to a fence he knew and get the best price possible. The tea set would fetch a sizable amount of money, but the letters would give him the cash he needed. He knew a collector who was willing to pay him well for that merchandise.

"Time to get busy, the day is passing and I need to get as much money as I can."

Looking in his rearview mirror, he pulled away from the curb and headed to Boston to his favorite fence to get rid of all Susanna's ill-gotten goods.

Chapter 18

The police station was typical of any small town's. It housed the station, the jail, the court and several municipal offices. The police department and small detaining cells were situated downstairs. The detective squad was to the left of the dispatcher's area and was bustling at this hour of the morning.

Detective Maher was sitting at his desk, reading the report on the vandalism and robbery of Susanna Smith's home the night before. The fingerprints that had been found were being run through the system. Susanna Smith would have to let them take her prints to determine if there were prints other than hers. She could do this when she came in to give her report.

There was something odd about the report he was reading, Maher thought. Susanna Smith had been in town less than a week. The house had been vacant over a year. If someone was going to rob the house, it should have been then, not now. The malicious way in which things were destroyed or broken showed a personal attack and rage. Whoever did this was angry. But why were they angry? The person or persons doing this also knew the house and knew Susanna Smith. Of this he was sure. He was going to have to go through the whole prior week with her to see if he could find a link.

As he was mulling this over, the telephone rang to tell him that Susanna Smith and William Shaw were here to see him. He looked up to see them walking through the door.

"Miss Smith, Mr. Shaw, please, both of you come and sit down. I didn't expect to see you, Mr. Shaw."

"Detective Maher, Mr. Shaw was my aunt's attorney and has been handling her estate for me. We were supposed to go somewhere today and he came to the house to pick me up. When he saw what had happened, he felt he should come here with me. Is there a problem?"

"No problem. I'm glad you have somebody to help you. I would like to go through the series of events since your arrival. It is my belief that someone you met or talked to this week may have been responsible for what happened last night. I would also like to get your fingerprints so that we can see which are yours and which might be our felon or felons. Could we do that step first?"

"Why don't you do that and get it over with, Susanna. That way, they can get started looking though the system and maybe find the culprits," William Shaw said with authority, and Susanna was led off to get the task done.

"Detective Maher, while Ms. Smith is gone I would like to tell you something she told me. She is worried about getting someone in trouble, but I believe it is relevant for you to know this information. As you know, Susanna's aunt left the home and contents to her in her will. This past week she has been trying to decide what to do with these things and has been getting estimates and appraisals. My son has been handling the real estate portion, but he brought in a college friend by the name of Jerry Carter to look at the contents and see what might be done at an estate sale. Susanna had a run-in with Mr. Carter on Thursday and it got a little heated. You see, Susanna has very old, valuable letters that he wants, and she has refused to sell them to him."

"Were the letters stolen last night? asked Detective Maher.

"No, Susanna had put them in the car in a recessed area where they could not be seen. She had also taken her dog with her. We had dinner together last night along with my son and Mary Connors, the town librarian."

"That may explain why the house was so torn apart. Obviously, the felon didn't find what he wanted. If this proves to be the case, he or she may come back again, and this time someone could get hurt. Why would this Jerry Carter do this? He certainly could go through legitimate means to obtain the letters."

"Jerry has had gambling issues in the past. Look Detective, I'm not saying Jerry did this, I'm only saying I think you might want to look into this matter."

Before the detective could reply, Susanna returned from being fingerprinted. She wiped her hands on a towelette to remove the remnants of the test still on her fingers.

"Well that was messy. Isn't there a better way to do this?"

"Actually there is, but it's not available in our little town. Now, can you reconstruct for me what has happened since you arrived in Weymouth?"

Susanna told the day-by-day account of her week. Included in this report were all the people she met and all the places she had been. She also related the same story about Jerry Carter that Mr. Shaw had given. Her retelling however, gave a more complete account of how uncomfortable Susanna felt with the situation. She also gave the detective a list of what she knew to be missing.

"We will type up the inventory from the list that you gave us and, when it's ready, ask you to sign off on it. Can you please wait while we do this?" he asked.

"Yes, we'll wait. I'd like to get as much done today as possible."

Bill Maher got up from the desk and walked across the room to an associate sitting at a desk. He handed over the list to the young man who began working on the inventory report. Coming back to his desk, he had a concerned look on his face.

When he sat down, he looked at Susanna and commented, "I think this warrants my checking into Jerry Carter's background and character as well as his whereabouts last night. I need to warn you, however, to be careful. If he did do this and did not get what he wanted, he may come back, and this time might hurt someone. I think you should consider staying somewhere else, with someone if possible."

"Detective, I have tried. She is a stubborn woman. I will try to get up with my son and see if he can come by and help. I will also do my best to watch out for Susanna until we find out who did this."

"That would be great, Mr. Shaw. I will continue to have the patrol car come by and check out the area on a regular basis."

"I don't want you to do that, Mr. Shaw. John is away and I don't want you to ruin his weekend. I want you to promise me you won't contact him. Detective Maher, a neighbor of mine from New Jersey came up to stay with me, so someone will be in the house. Mrs. O'Hara and I will be very careful and we will let the patrol car know if something is wrong. How about we arrange a signal? I will leave the porch light on, and if for some reason the light is out, they can come in and check on us."

"I can arrange that, but I'm going on record to say I don't like it, Ms. Smith."

With all this arranged, and after signing off on the inventory list, Susanna and William Smith left the police station and returned to the house and Mrs. O'Hara's scones and hot tea.

Chapter 19

When Susanna and Mr. Shaw arrived back at the house, they were astonished at how much Mrs. O'Hara had accomplished in such a short period of time. The parlor had been cleaned of the broken glass and the books were back on the shelves. The furniture was back in position and the tables where they belonged. The pictures had all been placed on top of the piano, minus the frames, beginning with Susanna's baby pictures. The kitchen was almost completely back in order, and hot tea and scones were waiting for them.

Quincy greeted both of them with wet kisses and sprinkles of flour on his muzzle.

"Mrs. O'Hara, you've been busy. It looks like Quincy's been busy too!"

"Oh Darlin', he's been his helpful self. I tried to clean up a wee bit and put things back in order, but they might not be in the right place. At least they're put away and off the floor. How did you make out?"

"I gave my report and they took my fingerprints. They'll also get the report back about the other fingerprints taken at the scene. Hopefully, the police will come up with a match and find out who did this."

"You've been through a shock! Both of you sit down and have some hot tea with lots of sugar and milk. That always perks me up and I know it will do the same for the two of you. Have some scones as well. I didn't have time to go out and get cream, so you will have to make do with some peach preserves from the pantry."

Sitting at the kitchen nook, William Shaw and Susanna enjoyed the tea and scones with relish. They shared a quiet moment as they looked out at the gazebo, admiring the fruit trees, which were full of buds and ready to bloom. William Shaw looked over at Mrs. O'Hara and saw her looking at Susanna with a concerned look.

"Mrs. O'Hara won't you please sit down and join us. You've been very busy. You must be tired," he said softly.

"I think I will join you for a cup of tea."

"Susanna, I think you've had quite a night. Your morning has been busy, too. You must be exhausted. I know we were supposed to go to the Adams Homestead today, but I think we should postpone it. They're open tomorrow, and if you feel up to it we can go then. Mrs. O'Hara, perhaps you would like to join us as well. And I'd really like to take you both to lunch at the Ivy Inn. What do you think?"

"Mr. Shaw, please call me Margaret. I would like to join you but I think I will stay here and make myself useful. It is, however, a good idea for Susanna to go with you and get out of here for a while. It will take her mind off of things and give her an outing. Quincy can stay with me so that you won't worry about him, Susanna."

"Mrs. O'Hara, I can't leave you with this mess while I go out enjoying myself," said Susanna.

"Yes, you can and you will! Mr. Shaw, it's settled. You two go and I won't hear another word about it." She said this with so much authority that William Shaw and Susanna looked at her with surprise.

"Margaret, I will take Susanna if you do one thing for me."

"What do you want me to do?" asked Mrs. O'Hara.

"Call me William."

They were all laughing now and the conversation moved to more pleasant topics. Susanna agreed to go the next day, but only if Mrs. O'Hara would be careful, and keep the porch light on as agreed with Detective Maher. Susanna would also let the detective know what her plans were for the day and give him her cell phone number in case he needed to reach her.

"Susanna, where do you have the old letters? Did you take them with you to the police station this morning? Are they in the house or the car?" questioned Mr. Shaw.

"I brought them in last night. I was afraid to leave them in the car. I left them here this morning with Mrs. O'Hara and Quincy. I felt they would be safer. Would you like to see them?"

"I would like to see them, but not today. I was just wondering where they were. I'm thinking they're probably safe in the house for now, but I think on Tuesday you might want to place them in a safer place, such as a safe deposit box. If the letters were what the thief or thieves were looking for and didn't find, they might come back, and this time it might be worse. Please, think about it.

"Well, I'd best be going. I'll pick you up tomorrow at nine. If you need help, or if you want to stay at my house, please give me a call. Have a good day, both of you. I can see myself out."

"William, please come for breakfast tomorrow before the two of you go out. I make great pancakes—there are some peaches I can put in them. Come around eight and bring your appetite," Mrs. O'Hara said with a twinkle in her eyes and an impish grin on her face.

"That's a date. See you then."

William Shaw left them sitting there and walked to the door. Before leaving he checked to make sure the porch light was on. Satisfied, he walked out the door, locking it behind him. He got into his car and had a troubled mind about this whole affair. Looking back at the house, he felt sure that the thief would return. He picked up his cell phone and made a call.

Chapter 20

As William Shaw was making his telephone call, Jerry Carter was sitting in his car on the opposite side of the street, a half block down from Susanna's house. He could see the Durango parked in the driveway, as well as two other cars. He knew the one car, the Mercedes, belonged to John's father. Jerry observed William Shaw leaving the house and saw him making a call. A minute or two later, he saw him pull away. Jerry wondered who the other car belonged to. As he was pondering his next move and whether he should make a run for the house, a patrol car came down the street. Thinking it wise to leave the area, he waited for the patrol car to go by and then pulled away from the curb.

Three hours earlier Jerry had been in a seedy part of Boston meeting with his fence and later on with his collector. He had managed to get about $75,000 for all the antiques and articles he had taken from the house. The silver had fetched a nice price from his collector. They discussed the letters and Jerry knew that once they were in the collector's hands he would be able to clear up his gambling debts and have enough money left to tide him over for a while. All he needed were those letters!

While on the earlier trip, Jerry also visited a small bodega. There, he was given an address where he met someone who for a price supplied him with an unregistered, unmarked, nine-millimeter semi-automatic gun. Remembering this purchase, he reached to the glove compartment and opened it, reassuring himself that the gun was still there. Needing support and worried that he might have trouble with his bookie the next day, he touched the cold metal and felt secure.

"At least I won't go unprepared in case there's trouble. I think I might need this when I go after the letters as well. Susanna Smith will not give them up easily, and then there's that mutt. I will go back later and case the house. I need to see when I can get back inside. Maybe I'll have some luck and the house will be empty. I better wait until its dark," he said out loud. He was trying to convince himself that it would all go just as planned.

He found a safe place to hide and fell asleep in anticipation of what the night might hold.

Chapter 21

The afternoon was a busy time for Susanna and Mrs. O'Hara. They worked as a team and by suppertime the house was livable again. Most of the damage had been cleaned up and the rest Mrs. O'Hara would take care of the next day. Both of them had had little sleep and after their day of hard physical labor, were extremely tired. Sitting at the kitchen nook, relaxing, they were trying to decide what to do for dinner.

"Let me take you out to dinner Mrs. O'Hara. It's the least I can do for all your help."

"Oh Darlin', don't be silly. A wee bit of work 'tis all it was. I really think we should relax and stay in. I found some eggs in the fridge and with some other bits and pieces I can make us both lovely omelets. I have some scones left over and have already made shortbread cookies that we can have for dessert. If you can find a dram of wine, we will be set. Besides, it will give us time to chat. I also think we can both use a good night's sleep. My mum always said everything is better after our tummies are full and we get our rest. So, what do you say?"

"Sounds good to me, Mrs. O'Hara."

Quincy had been patient all day—even through the vacuuming. The vacuum was not one of his favorite machines. He had found a good place to hide during all this activity, but now he was hungry and would not be ignored. He sat in front of Susanna and placed his paw on her leg. He was not going away until he was fed.

"Okay, boy. I know, you've been patient, but now it's your time. I'll tell you what, let me feed you now and when you're finished, I'll take you for a nice long walk. We'll get out of Mrs. O'Hara's hair and give her time to get dinner together. What do you think about that?"

Whether Quincy knew what she said or it was the soothing way she talked to him, he went right to his food dish, which Susanna promptly filled. She then patiently waited for Quincy to finish. When he was done, she did exactly what she said she would and they went for a long walk.

By the time they got back, Mrs. O'Hara had the omelets ready and on the table. The aroma of the food hit Susanna as soon as she walked in the door. She realized how famished she was and how grateful that Mrs. O'Hara was there.

"This looks wonderful, Mrs. O'Hara! I don't know how I would have gotten through this day without you. Thank you so much for coming."

"It has been my pleasure to help you. Now, let's eat."

It was an enjoyable dinner. For a moment Susanna forgot about the events of the day. She was very comfortable with Mrs. O'Hara and looked to her for her motherly advice. Susanna's own mother had been quiet, reserved, and very intellectual. Mrs. O'Hara had an earthiness and warmth about her. Her emotions were written all over her, and she spoke her mind. The only thing both women had in common was their love and caring for Susanna.

"Darlin', how are you really? Have you made up your mind as to what you're going to do with this house?"

"It's been an emotional roller coaster since the day I got to Weymouth. Memories have come back that were long ago forgotten. Also, guilt has been my constant companion. I realized last week how self-absorbed I've been. I thought I was very independent and could do everything myself. Now I know that the support of family and friends is the most important thing in life. Unfortunately, it's too late. My family is gone. I'm all that's left," she said, with such sadness that Mrs. O'Hara felt a tear on her cheek.

"Darlin', don't be so hard on yourself. Your family may be gone, but you have good friends who care about you, both old and new. I believe your aunt Susanna knew what she was doing by leaving this house and her mementos to you. She made you come here and face your past. She helped you to connect with your family and showed you that you have a future. She's reaching out to you from the grave and showing you the way."

"I have to tell you, Mrs. O'Hara, I've been very happy here. I've been thinking about how I might relocate. What do you think I should do?"

"I can't answer that for you. That is a decision only you can make. I don't want you to move, but I'm being a wee bit selfish. You must do what is right for you."

Mrs. O'Hara looked at Susanna sadly and realized that she had already made up her mind, she just didn't know it yet. She thought about how much she would miss Susanna. Not being able to see her every day would be difficult, but she would learn to adjust and she could always come here to visit. It just wouldn't be the same.

"Darlin' its nine o'clock and I'm very tired. I need to go to bed. I have a lot of things to finish up tomorrow. You have an early day as well. You should try to get some sleep, too."

"I will, Mrs. O'Hara. You go ahead. I think I'll read some more of the old letters before I go to the Adams Homestead tomorrow. I also have to walk Quincy one more time before

I go to bed. I won't make it late. I'm tired myself, and it's been a busy twenty-four hours. Goodnight. See you in the morning."

"Sweet dreams."

As Susanna was coming out of the house with Quincy for his last walk of the evening, the patrol car drove by. It stopped and the policemen talked with her and asked if everything was okay. They agreed to stay where they were until she finished her walk and was safely back in the house. Once finished with the business at hand, both Susanna and Quincy returned home and locked the door behind them, making sure the porch light was properly turned on and working.

The patrolmen, satisfied, drove off. They stopped further down the road and spoke to someone in a Jeep Cherokee for a few moments and then left to complete their rounds.

Chapter 22

Dearest Friend   *Braintree July 12, 1775*

I have met with some abuse and very Ill treatment. I want you for my protector and justifier.

In this Day of distress for our Boston Friends when everyone does what in them lyes to serve them, your Friend Gorge Trott and family moved up to Braintree, went in with her two Brothers and families with her Father, but they not thinking themselves so secure as further in the Country moved away. After they were gone Mr. Church took the house and took a number of borders. Mr. Trott had engaged a house near his Friends but being prevented going quite so soon as he designd, and the great distress people were in for houses, the owner had taken in a family and dissappointed Mr. Trott, nor could he procure a house any where, for the more remote from the sea coast you go the thicker you find the Boston people. After this dissappointment, he had his Goods without unloading brought back to Braintree, and he with all his family were obliged to shelter themselves in your Brothers house till he could seek further. You know, from the situation of my Brothers family it was impossible for them to tarry there, Mrs. Trots circumstances requiring more rooms than one. In this extremity he applied to me to see if I would not accommodate him with the next house, every other spot in Town being full. I sent for Mr. Hayden and handsomely asked him, he said he would try, but he took no pains to procure himself a place. There were several in the other parish which were to be let, but my Gentlemen did not chuse to go there. Mr. Trot upon account of his Buisness which is in considered demand wanted to be here. Mr. Trott, finding there was no hopes of his going out said he would go in with him, provided I would let him have the chamber I improved for a Dairy room and the lower room and chamber over it which Hayden has. I then sent and asked Mr. Hayden to be so kind as to remove his things into the other part of the house and told him he might improve the kitchen and back chamber, the bed room and the Dairy room in which he already had a bed. He would not tell me whether he would or not, but said I was turning him out of Door to oblige Boston folks, and he could not be stired up, and if you was at home you would not once ask him to go out, but was more of a Gentlemen. (You must know that both his Sons are in the army, not but one Days Work has been done by any of them this Spring.) I as mildly as I could represented the distress of Mr. Trot and the difficulties to which he had been put—that I looked upon it my Duty to do all in my power to Oblige him—and that he Hayden would be much better accommodated than hundred who were turnd out of Town—and I finally said that Mr. Trott should go in. In this State, Sister Adams got to bed and then there was not a Spot in Brothers house for them to lie down in. I removed my dairy things, and once more requested the old Man to move into the other part of the house, but he positively tells me he will not and all the art of Man shall not stir him, even dares me to put any article out of one room into an other. Says Mr. Trot shall not come in—he has got possession and he will keep it. What not have a place to entertain his children in when they come to see him. I now write you an account of the matter, and desire you to write to him and give me orders what course I shall take. I must take Mr. Trott in with me and all his family for the present, till he can look out further or have that house. It would make your heart ake to see what difficulties and distresses the poor Boston people are driven to. Belcher has two families with him. There are 3 in Veses [Veasey's] house, 2 in Etters, 2 in Mr. Savils, 2 in Jonathan Bass'es and yet that obstinate Wretch will not remove his few things into the other part of that house, but live there paying no rent upon the distresses of others.

It would be needless to enumerate all his impudence. Let it suffice to say it moved me so much that I had hard Work to suppress my temper. I want to know whether his things may be removed into the other part of the house, whether he consents or not? Mr. Trott would rejoice to take the whole, but would put up with any thing rather than be a burden to his Friends. I told the old Man I believed I was doing nothing but what I should be justified in. He *says well tis a time of war get him out if I can, but cannon Ball shall not move him. If you think you are able to find 3 houses, for 3 such tenents as you have they must abide where they are, tho I own I shall be much mortified if you do not support me.*

I feel too angry to make this any thing further than a Letter of Buisness, I am most sincerely yours, (22)

Abigail Adams

Letter in hand, Susanna wondered what had happened to Josiah Quincy. Nothing was mentioned in this letter, although Abigail did sound a little flustered.

Perhaps there was more information in the next letter, she thought. What a distressing time for Abigail. This "Hayden" sounded like a typical stubborn New Englander. Susanna had to see how she made out.

Dearest Friend *Braintree July 16 1775*

I have this afternoon had the pleasure of receiving your Letter by your Friends Mr. Collins and Kaighn and an English Gentle man his Name I do not remember. It was next to seeing my dearest Friend. Mr. Collins could tell me more perticuliarly about you and your Health than I have been able to hear since you left me. I rejoice in his account of your better Health, and of your spirits, tho he says I must not expect to see you till next spring. I hope he does not speak the truth. I know (I think I do, for am not I your Bosome Friend?) your feelings, your anxieties, your exertions, &c. [etc.] more than those before whom you are obliged to wear the face of chearfulness.

I have seen your Letters to Col. Palmer and Warren. I pity your Embaresments. How difficult the task to quench out the fire and the pride of private ambition, and to sacrifice ourselfs and all our hopes and expectations to the publick weal. How few have souls capable of so noble an undertaking—how often are the laurels worn by those who have had no share in earning them, but there is a future recompence of reward to which the upright man looks, and which he will most assuredly obtain provided he perserveres unto the end.—The appointment of the Generals Washington and Lee, gives universal satisfaction. The people have the highest opinion of Lees abilities, but you know the continuation of the popular Breath, depends much upon favorable events.

I had the pleasure of seeing both the Generals and their Aid de camps soon after their arrival and of being personally made known to them. They very politely express their regard for you. Major Miflin said he had orders from you to visit me at Braintree. I told him I should be very happy to see him there, and accordingly sent Mr. Thaxter to Cambridge with a card to him and Mr. Read [Reed] to dine with me. Mrs. Warren and her Son were to be with me. They very politely received the Message and lamented that they were not able to upon account of Expresses which they were that day to get in readiness to send of.

I was struck with General Washington. You had prepaired me to entertain a favorable opinion of him, but I thought the one half was not told me. Dignity with ease, and complacency, the Gentleman and Soldier look agreeably blended in him. Modesty marks every line and feture of his face. Those lines of Dryden instantly occurd to me.

> "Mark his Majestick fabrick! he's a temple
> Sacred by birth, and built by hands divine
> His Souls the Deity that lodges there
> Nor is the pile unworthy of the God."

General Lee looks like a careless hardy Veteran and from his appearance brought to my mind his namesake Charls the 12, king of Sweeden. The Elegance of his pen far exceeds that of his person. I was much pleased with your Friend Collins. I persuaded them to stay coffe with me, and he was as unreserved and social as if we had been old acquaintances, and said he was very loth to leave the house. I would have detain them till morning, but they were very desirous of reaching Cambridge.

Major Miflin told me of your orders about Josiah Quincy. I agree—I will write no more of him, I know you are doing something and that is enouf—The Major will let me know when the orders have been carred out. [I]*

You have made often and frequent complaints that your Friends do not write to you. I have stired up some of them. Dr. Tufts, Col. Quincy, Mr. Tudor, Mr. Thaxter all have wrote you now, and a Lady whom I am willing you should value preferable to all others save one. May not I in my turn make complaints? All the Letters I receive from you seem to be wrote in so much haste, that they scarcely leave room for a social feeling. They let me know that you exist, but some of them contain scarcely six lines. I want some sentimental Effusions of the Heart.

*(I) See Chapter Notes.

I am sure you are not destitute of them or are they all absorbed in the great publick. Much is due to that I know, but being part of the whole I lay claim to a Larger Share than I have had. You used to be more communicative a Sundays. I always loved a Sabeth days letter, for then you had a greater command of your time—but hush to all complaints.

I am surprized that you have not been more accurately informd of what passes in the camps. As to intelegance from Boston, tis but very seldom we are able to collect any thing that may be relied upon, and to report the vague flying rumours would be endless. I heard yesterday by one Mr. Rolestone [Roulstone] a Goldsmith who got out in a fishing Schooner, that there distress encreased upon them fast, their Beaf is all spent, their Malt and Sider all gone, to all the fresh provisions they can procure they are obliged to give to the sick and wounded. 19 of our Men who were in Jail and were wounded at the Battle of Charlstown were Dead. No Man dared now to be seen talking to his Friend in the Street, they were obliged to be within every evening at ten o'clock according to Martial Law, nor could any inhabitant walk any Street in Town after that time without a pass from Gage. He has orderd all the melasses to be stilld up into rum for the Soldiers, taken away all Licences, and given out others obligeing to a forfeiture of ten pounds LM if any rum is sold without written orders from the General. He give much the same account of the kill'd and wounded we have had from others. The Spirit he says which prevails among the Soldiers is a Spirit of Malice and revenge, there is no true courage and bravery to be observed among them. their Duty is hard allways mounting guard with their packs at their back ready for an alarm which they live in continued hazard of. Doctor Eliot is not on bord a man of war, as has been reported, but perhaps was left in Town as the comfort and support of those who cannot escape. he was constantly with our prisoners. Mr. Lovel and Leach with others are certainly in Jail. A poor Milch cow was last week kill'd in Town and sold for a shilling stearling per pound. The transports arrived last week from York, but every additional Man adds to their distress.—There has been a little Expidition this week to Long Island. There has been before several attempts to go on but 3 men of war lay near, and cutters all round the Island that they could not succeed. A number of whale boats lay at Germantown; 300 volenters commanded by one Capt. Tupper came on monday evening and took the boats, went on and brought of 70 odd Sheep, 15 head of cattle, and 16 prisoners 13 of whom were sent by Simple Sapling to mow the Hay which they had very badly executed. They were all a sleep in the house and barn when they were taken. There were 3 women with them. Our Heroes came of in triumph not being observed by their Enimies. This spirited up other[s]. They could not endure the thought that the House and barn should afford them any shelter. They did not distroy them the night before for fear of being discovered. Capt. Wild of this Town with about 25 of his company, Capt. Gold [Gould] of Weymouth with as many of his, and some other volenters to the amount of an 100, obtaind leave to go on and destroy the Hay together with the House and barn and in open day in full view of the men of war they set of from the Moon so call'd covered by a number of men who were placed there, went on, set fire to the Buildings and Hay. A number of armed cutters immediately Surrounded the Island, fired upon our Men. They came of [off] with a hot and continued fire upon them, the Bullets flying in every direction and the Men of Wars boats plying them with small arms. Many in this Town who were spectators expected every moment our Men would all be sacrificed, for sometimes they were so near as to be calld to and damnd by their Enimies and orderd to surrender yet they all returnd in safty, not one Man even wounded. Upon the Moon we lost one Man from the cannon on board the Man of War. On the Evening of the same day a Man of War came and anchord near Great Hill, and two cutters came to Pig Rocks. It occasiond an alarm in this Town and we were up all Night. They remain there yet, but have not ventured to land any men.

This Town have chosen their Representative. Col. Palmer is the Man. There was a considerable musture upon Thayers side, and Vintons company marched up in order to assist, but got sadly disappointed. Newcomb insisted upon it that no man should vote who was in the army—he had no notion of being under the Military power—said we might be so situated as to have the greater part of the people engaged in the Military, and then all power would be wrested out of the hands of the civil Majestrate. He insisted upon its being put to vote, and carried his point immediately. It brought Thayer to his Speach who said all he could against it.—As to the Situation of the camps, our Men are in

Dear John

general Healthy, much more so at Roxbury than Cambridge, and the Camp in vastly better order. General Thomas has the character of an Excelent officer. His Merit has certainly been over-look'd as modest merrit generally is. I hear General Washington is much pleased with his conduct.

Every article here in the West India way is very scarce and dear. In six weeks [s] we shall not be able to purchase any article of the kind. I wish you would let Bass get me one pound of peper, and 2 yd. of black caliminco for Shooes. I cannot wear leather if I go bare foot the reason I need not mention. Bass may make a fine profit if he layes in a stock for himself. You can hardly immagine how much we want many common small articles which are not manufactured amongst ourselves, but we will have them in time. Not one pin is to be purchased for love nor money. I wish you could convey me a thousand by any Friend travelling this way. Tis very provoking to have such a plenty so near us, but tantulus like not able to touch. I should have been glad to have laid in a small stock of the West India articles, but I cannot get one copper. No person thinks of paying any thing, and I do not chuse to run in debt. I endeavor to live in the most frugal manner possible, but I am many times distressed—Mr. Trot I have accommodated by removeing the office into my own chamber, and after being very angry and sometimes persuaideding I obtain the mighty concession of the Bed room, but I am now so crouded as not to have a Lodging for a Friend that calls to see me. I must beg you would give them warning to seek a place before Winter. Had that house been empty I could have had an 100 a year for it. Many person [s] had applied before Mr. Trot, but I wanted some part of it my self, and the other part it seems I have no command of.——We have since I wrote you had many fine showers, and altho the crops of grass have been cut short, we have a fine prospect of Indian corn and English grain. Be not afraid, ye beasts of the field, for the pastures of the Wilderness do spring, the Tree beareth her fruit, the vine and the olive yeald their increase.

We have not yet been much distressed for grain. Every thing at present looks blooming. O that peace would once more extend her olive Branch.

> "This Day be Bread and peace my lot
> All Else beneath the Sun
> Thou knowst if best bestowed or not
> And let thy will be done."
>
> But is the Almighty ever bound to please
> Ruild by my wish or studious of my ease.
> Shall I determine where his frowns shall fall
> And fence my Grotto from the Lot of all?
> Prostrate his Sovereign Wisdom I adore
> Intreat his Mercy, but I dare no more."

Our little ones send Duty to pappa. You would smile to see them all gather round mamma upon the reception of a letter to hear from pappa, and Charls with open mouth, What does par say—did not he write no more. And little Tom says I wish I could see par. Upon Mr. Rice's going into the army he asked Charls if he should get him a place, he catchd at it with great eagerness and insisted upon going. We could not put him of, he cryed and beged, no *obstical we could raise was sufficient to satisfy him, till I told him he must first obtain your consent. Then he insisted that I must write about it, and has been every day these 3 weeks insisting upon my asking your consent. At last I have promised to write to you, and am obliged to be as good as my word.—I have now wrote you all I can collect from every quarter. Tis fit for no eye but yours, because you can make all necessary allowances. I cannot coppy.*

There are yet in Town 4 of the Selectman and some thousands of inhabitants tis said.—I hope to hear from you soon. Do let me know if there is any prospect of seeing you? Next Wedensday is 13 weeks since you went away.

I must bid you adieu. You have many Friends tho they have not noticed you by writing. I am sorry they have been so neglegent. I hope no share of that blame lays upon your most affectionate (23)
Portia

"Wow, Quincy, what interesting times. I wonder how she managed. Women have a hard enough time today to be heard. I know how Abigail felt, though. Just try being a woman today and deal with an auto mechanic. They think women are stupid. How typical that Hayden wouldn't do something a woman asked."

Susanna looked at her companion; there was no response. Quincy was sound asleep on the rug. He'd had a busy twenty-four hours too! She then realized how tired she was herself. It was almost eleven and there was a busy day planned for tomorrow. Susanna placed all of the letters back in their box and decided to take them with her tomorrow. She would keep them upstairs with her tonight and insist upon using her car tomorrow, where they could be locked up unseen.

"Quincy, let's go to bed."

Chapter 23

Jerry Carter roused himself from a deep sleep. Looking at his watch, he saw that it was nine o'clock in the evening. He was groggy and disoriented. He was afraid to go home and get cleaned up. He didn't know whether the police, or worse, Joey might be there. Better to stay away, he thought. He decided to go to a nearby eatery, get some food and use the facilities. When he finished, he would head over to Susanna's house and see what the situation was, and when he might be able to get inside and find the letters. First, he would check the car. If those letters weren't there, he would have to go back inside to get them.

At eleven, Jerry drove by the Smith house. Two cars were still in the driveway. The Durango was there, but he didn't know who belonged to the blue Saturn. "She must have someone staying with her. I wonder who it is," he mused. He drove down the street and turned around, coming back to park a little way down from house. He turned off his lights and sat watching the house. The lights were still on in the bedroom upstairs, and the porch light was on. Within a few minutes the upstairs light went out.

"I'm going to have to find a way to get rid of that porch light before I look in the car. I don't want anybody seeing me. I'll wait here for an hour and make sure they're asleep. Then I'll check things out," he thought.

At midnight, Jerry was ready. Just as he touched the car door handle, he saw lights coming down the street. He quickly moved to his right and lay down on the front seat.

The car drove by slowly and, when it had passed, Jerry got up to look. It was a police car patrolling the area. He thought he'd better wait to see if it would come back before he made his move.

Waiting impatiently, he almost got out again when he saw a neighbor walking his dog. It happened to be a big dog, so he cautiously remained in the car. Ten minutes later, he saw this same neighbor go back into his house. It was now almost twelve-thirty, and he needed to do something quick, but what! The house was definitely being monitored and, if a police car was patrolling outside, then a policeman might be inside. If they thought he was involved, they might already know about his car. Almost frantic now, Jerry tried to decide the best thing to do. He had to meet Joey tomorrow at one o'clock with the money. In order to get the money he had to have the merchandise and get to the collector no later than eleven.

"I can't take the chance they'll trace me to this car. I better get rid of it and get another. I'll come back later when I do," he decided.

He quickly started the car and took off in search of another vehicle.

Chapter 24

"Bill, there's been a match on a set of fingerprints taken at the Smith house."

Detective Maher, on duty again, looked up from the paperwork on his desk.

"Who is it?"

"See for yourself," said the night sergeant.

Maher took the paper from the sergeant's hands and had to admit he wasn't surprised.

"Danny, find out where Jerry Carter is right now. Also, see if you can get information on the kind of car he has and his plates. I want to pick him up as quickly as possible before he can do any more damage. Call out to the car patrolling the Smith house and have the men be extra careful. Give them the make, model and plate number when you get it."

Detective Maher was deciding whether or not to contact Susanna Smith with this information when he realized how late it was. He decided to call her early in the morning so that she could at least be forewarned. Maybe they'd have Jerry in custody before he had to make that call. He did, however, make one telephone call before he went back to the papers on his desk.

Chapter 25

Sunday dawned sunny and warmer than the past week. Lying in bed, Susanna thought about the upcoming day and how much she was looking forward to it. Having read some of Abigail's letters, she wanted to see where everything had occurred so many years ago. Susanna knew she finally belonged somewhere and for once felt her birthright.

It was six-thirty and she was hungry. She also knew Quincy felt the same way. He was pacing and patiently waiting for her to get up. Mr. Shaw would be there in a little over an hour and her day would truly begin.

"Come on, handsome, I'll take you for a walk and feed you. Then, I have to get dressed. Let's get snapping!" she said with such exuberance that Quincy tilted his head to look at her.

Mrs. O'Hara was already in the kitchen, putting together her wonderful pancake batter. The aroma of coffee was filling the house and she was singing softly a melody that was unfamiliar to Susanna. The tune was definitely Irish and she would have to remember to ask Mrs. O'Hara what it was.

"Good morning. My, have you been busy. Did you sleep okay?" asked Susanna.

"That I did! Isn't it a glorious day? The coffee is almost ready. Take the little one for his walk and by the time you come back breakfast will be waiting for you."

"Okay! Let's go, Quincy."

The street was very quiet at this hour of the morning. It was the Sunday morning of Memorial Day weekend. Susanna wondered about her neighbors and hoped she would get to meet them soon. She also wondered if any of them were home or if they were all away for the weekend. Susanna noticed the houses on the street and realized what a nice, well-maintained neighborhood she was in. The lawns were trimmed and neat, the houses looked like they were freshly painted, and there was a feeling of peace. A little further down the street, Susanna noticed a car that definitely looked out place. It was older and had rusted out in spots. The right side front fender was hanging on precariously. How odd. In this neighborhood! "Oh well, maybe it belongs to a neighbor's child. I think we should get this walk over with and go get some coffee, Quincy," she said.

Chapter 26

Jerry Carter had had a bad night. First, he had to find a place to stash his car. This he did on the outskirts of Boston, near the water by an abandoned warehouse. He made sure to take his nine-millimeter with him before he left the car there. Then, he had to walk a distance to find a car he could steal to get back to Weymouth. He had just been back for a few minutes before he saw Susanna walk out of the house with Quincy. He ducked down quickly before she could see him.

"What a night! I'm running out of time. I'll wait until she gets back inside and then make my move. Here she comes and here comes the police car again. Damn! I just can't win!"

Calculating time, he figured out that the patrol made its rounds every hour on the hour, so he had time between now and the next patrol. The patrol car stopped to talk to Susanna, and he realized that they were checking in.

"Ms. Smith, how are you this morning. Did you have a quiet night?"

"Yes I did, officer. I hope you had the same," she replied.

"Not bad. Listen, Detective Maher wanted me to tell you that the fingerprints lifted at your house turned out to be that of Jerry Carter. He wants you to be careful and on the alert. He said to tell you he'd call you this morning and give you a status report. We'll still patrol every hour until that guy's in custody. If you have any problems, make sure to turn the porch light out. Keep your telephone handy as well. Well, hope you have a nice day!"

"Thank you. You do the same."

Susanna watched them go down the street. What had started out as a great day was losing its charm. As she started to open the door, a car pulled into the driveway. It was Mr. Shaw and he was an hour early. He looked concerned and Susanna hoped everything was all right.

"Mr. Shaw, you're early. Is everything okay?"

"I thought I would come early. Detective Maher called me to let me know the news. Have you heard?"

"Yes, the police car just left. Please come in."

As they went into the kitchen, the telephone was ringing. Susanna ran to pick it up.

"Hello."

"Ms. Smith, this is Detective Maher."

"Hi, I just talked to one of your officers. He told me the fingerprints belong to Jerry Carter. Is this true?"

"Yes, that's why I'm calling. We're looking for him. He didn't go back to his apartment yesterday and his car is missing. Please be careful, and if you see anything strange please contact me. I'll let you know if we hear anything."

"Thanks, Detective Maher. Mr. Shaw is here and we were planning a day out, do you think we should postpone our outing?" she queried.

"I think if you're with Mr. Shaw and you have people around you, you'll be okay."

"Thanks, I'll talk with you later, detective. Good-bye."

Susanna hung up the phone and looked at Mr. Shaw and Mrs. O'Hara. By this time they were both staring at her with a questioning look.

"Detective Maher says it was Jerry Carter who ransacked the house and took the missing items. He wants us to be careful. He said not to postpone our tour, but maybe it would be a good idea. What do you think, Mr. Shaw?"

"I think we will go, and so will Mrs. O'Hara and Quincy. I'm not leaving anybody in this house today. Let's relax and have breakfast. Then head out for the Homestead," he replied.

"Oh no. I have too much to do here and you two need the day out. I'll be fine."

"No! You will come as well. Whatever it is you have to do can wait until tomorrow. That's the end of it! Now let's have something to eat, I'm starving," William Shaw said with such authority and conviction that Mrs. O'Hara conceded and nodded her head in agreement.

Chapter 27

Susanna couldn't stop shaking. She was still in shock over the violent events of the morning. Sitting in the waiting room of the local veterinarian, she was trying to piece together the sequence of what had occurred. How could it have happened?

Mrs. O'Hara came back into the waiting room and saw Susanna sitting there, shaking, with her arms folded and wrapped across her chest. Worry and pain were etched on Susanna's face, and Mrs. O'Hara's heart was aching for her. Coming over to her quietly, she placed a hand on Susanna's shoulder.

"Darlin,' please, drink this hot tea. You need it. Put this blanket around your shoulders, too, it will warm you up. You're in shock!"

Turning to Mrs. O'Hara, Susanna fell into her arms and, placing her head on the older woman's shoulder, sobbed uncontrollably. Mrs. O'Hara held her tight and softly tried to soothe her.

"Darlin', it will be all right. You'll see. Quincy will be fine. He'll make it through the surgery. He's a strong, healthy fellow. He's not ready to leave you yet. You both have many years ahead of you. Please, drink the tea. It will make you feel better. I'll stay with you and wait for the doctor."

Susanna pulled herself together and stopped crying. Leaning back against the wall and holding on to Mrs. O'Hara's hand, she began to sip the tea. Slowly, she focused on the events of the morning and wondered if there was anything she could have done differently to prevent this tragedy. She'd been smug, ignoring her inability to control the evil actions of others.

She'd felt almost untouchable, even with the break-in. How could she have been so stupid?

It was hard to believe that a day that had been so promising when she woke up this morning could have taken such a turn. It was only eleven, yet it seemed like hours since Jerry Carter caused her such heartbreak. Susanna couldn't remember if it was the crashing sound of the door being opened or the explosion of the gun, which first startled her. It all happened so quickly.

They had just sat down for breakfast. Mr. Shaw and Mrs. O'Hara were chatting away, planning the day, when a shattering sound from the front of the house caused them to start. Quincy had been patiently waiting for a tidbit from breakfast when the noise occurred. Jumping up, he flew to the front room barking and growling. Following him quickly, Susanna reached the front parlor in time to see Jerry Carter standing there with a gun in his hand. As Quincy came around the corner from the kitchen, Jerry Carter raised his gun directly at him. Quincy, following his instincts, lunged at Jerry in an effort to protect his mistress.

"Quincy! No!" cried Susanna.

Jerry fired the gun and the bullet hit Quincy in his chest. Quincy dropped to the floor immediately, unconscious.

"I don't want to hurt anybody else. Get those letters and be quick."

Susanna was frozen to the spot in which she had been standing. She could see that Quincy was still breathing, yet his blood was pooling under him. For some reason all she could do was stare, she couldn't move.

"I said get the letters!" demanded Carter.

By this time Mrs. O'Hara and Mr. Shaw were standing in the hall as well. Looking at the scene, Mr. Shaw was the first to speak.

"Susanna, get the letters. We need to take care of Quincy. The sooner Mr. Carter has them, the sooner he'll be gone," he said calmly, trying to diffuse the situation.

The words were no sooner out of his mouth than a form appeared behind Jerry. John Shaw came up from behind and hit Jerry over the head with a wrench. Sinking to the floor, Jerry Carter was finally subdued.

"I've called the police and they will be here shortly. Dad, find something to tie him up with while I check on Quincy. He's lost a lot of blood, but he's still breathing. He needs to get to a vet right away. He's too big for you to handle, so stay here and wait for the police. I'll take Quincy and Susanna. Hurry! I don't like the sound of his labored breathing."

"Susanna, do you have a blanket or sheet to carry him in? Susanna!"

Mrs. O'Hara realized that Susanna was in shock.

"Darlin', hurry, we must get him to the doctor. Quincy needs you."

Whether it was her words or the situation, Susanna finally roused. She and John wrapped Quincy in a sheet. John carried him to the Jeep and Susanna held his head, trying to soothe him.

"Such a good boy! Such a brave boy! Please, please, hold on! We're going to get you some help," she said almost in a whisper.

"John, how long before we get there? I don't like the way he sounds, and there's so much blood!"

"About five more minutes. Keep applying pressure to that wound. It will help with the bleeding. I used this vet before when I had Toby, my Golden. His name is Peter Marlow and he's very good. He keeps his office open on holidays for emergencies. If anybody can save Quincy, he can."

Fortunately, the office was close by. Dr. Marlow's office was small but was equipped for any type of emergency. When John pulled up in front of the building, Susanna jumped out of the car and rushed to the door. The door was locked and Susanna pounded hard. A man came running from the back. The waiting room, normally full of patients, was empty.

"Are you Dr. Marlow?"

"Yes, I am."

"Dr. Marlow, my dog's been shot. He's in the car, please help," cried Susanna.

Dr. Marlow followed Susanna and went to the Jeep. He recognized John and looked down at Quincy. The sheet was saturated with his blood.

"John, let me help you. Let's get him back to my surgery."

Gently placing the wounded dog on his table, the doctor examined him quickly.

"He's got blood in his lungs, and I don't know where the bullet is lodged. I will need to take x-rays, and I'm going to have to clear his lungs. Jane! Jane!" he yelled.

A woman in her mid-thirties came running into the room.

"Jane I need help. We have to move on this right away. Hurry! Let's get an x-ray."

"Are you the owner?"

"Yes, he's my dog."

"I will do the very best I can for him, but understand he's critically injured. What's his name?"

"His name's Quincy. Please help him. Don't let him die."

"I'm not sure how long this will take. Please wait outside and I'll come out and talk to you as soon as we know something."

"Can't I stay with him, I don't want him to be frightened." asked Susanna.

"Please, I can do this better and treat him faster without you here. Let me do my job. I promise you we will do everything to make him comfortable."

John took Susanna by the hand and led her out to the waiting room. He found her a seat and made sure she was settled. Then he called his father to find out what was going on at the house.

Chapter 28

William Shaw had taken control of the situation after John and Susanna left. Jerry Carter was still out cold, lying on the floor with his hands and feet tied with strips of sheeting. Mrs. O'Hara went into the kitchen to make a strong pot of coffee. The police and Detective Maher arrived within minutes of each other.

Bill Maher walked in and took in all that had occurred. He shook his head when he saw the gun and the blood stains on the floor. He quickly ordered an ambulance for Jerry Carter and turned to William Shaw.

"Who got shot? Where are Susanna Smith and your son?"

"Quincy, the poor fellow, got shot. This creature shot him after he broke in. Quincy was only protecting Susanna. How could he shoot him like that?" said Mrs. O'Hara who had just come back from the kitchen.

"Detective Maher, John and Susanna took him to the vet. He's in a poor condition. I hope he makes it."

"Please tell me the sequence of events. Start from when you got here until this happened."

The sound of William Shaw's cell phone ringing stopped his report. Flipping open the phone, William clicked it on.

"Dad, is everything okay?"

"John, the police are here. How's Quincy? How's Susanna? What's going on?"

"The vet is working on him right now. It doesn't look good, Dad. I'm worried about Susanna. She's still in shock. Do you think Detective Maher could have one of his men bring Mrs. O'Hara here? I think Susanna could use her support right now, especially if something happens to Quincy."

"Hold on, John."

Turning to the detective, William asked if this request was possible. Maher said it was not a problem, and when Mrs. O'Hara got there, would John please come back to the house. He wanted to talk to him. Hearing this, Mrs. O'Hara ran to collect her purse and sweater.

"John, they're walking out the door. Listen, when Mrs. O'Hara gets there please come back here, Bill Maher wants to talk to you."

"No problem, Dad, see you in a few minutes."

Chapter 29

Two hours had passed since John and Susanna arrived at the vet with Quincy. Mrs. O'Hara and Susanna were still sitting, waiting for word of his condition.

Standing up, Susanna began to pace back and forth.

"What's taking so long!" she cried.

"Darlin', it's a good thing. This means he hanging in there. Be patient, the doctor will come out and talk to you soon. You'll see."

As if on cue, the door opened and out walked Dr. Marlow.

"Dr. Marlow, how is he?"

"Quincy survived the surgery, but he's not out of the woods yet. The bullet lodged in his stomach. It caused a lot of internal bleeding and blood loss. Had the gun been aimed higher or had Quincy jumped differently, who knows what might have happened? If he makes it through the next twenty-four hours, he stands a good chance of surviving."

"Can I see him?"

"Jane is cleaning him up and making him comfortable. Please be aware that he's not looking very pretty right now. It might be a shock to see him like this, but he was a healthy dog before the shooting and this will be in his favor. Give Jane a few minutes and I'll take you back. After that, I suggest you go home and get some rest. I'll call you if anything happens."

Chapter 30

It had been a long day. By the time Susanna and Mrs. O'Hara got back to the house, the police were gone, Jerry Carter had been taken to the hospital, and the door had been somewhat hastily repaired. John and Mr. Shaw were sitting at the kitchen table waiting for them.

William Shaw watched them come in and looked at Susanna. She was ashen, weary, and worried. A lot had happened to this young lady in a short period of time. Not a good welcome to Weymouth. He hoped this wouldn't sour her on the town.

John stood up and pulled out chairs for them both. Susanna looked at him strangely, almost angrily, so much so that he wondered what was wrong.

"How's Quincy?" asked John.

"We won't know for twenty hours. If he makes it through the night, Dr. Marlow feels he'll survive."

"He'll make it Susanna," exclaimed John.

"Why would you care? It's because of you that he's in this condition. You didn't see Quincy, lying there with tubes and bandages, unconscious and at death's door. You brought

Jerry Carter into this house. You knew what he was like. How could you be friends with him? How could you allow this to happen?" snapped Susanna.

Both Mrs. O'Hara and Mr. Shaw looked at Susanna, surprised at this outburst.

"Darlin', surely John didn't know this would happen. You can't blame him for what Jerry Carter did."

"I can, and do, hold him responsible. Please leave my house, I don't want to see you again!" sobbed Susanna as she ran from the room and up the stairs to her bedroom.

John was stricken by the words. He watched her go and knew Susanna was right. He did know Jerry Carter, and it was his fault that all this had what happened. He had no right to be there. He stood up, looked at his father and Mrs. O'Hara, and without saying a word, turned, and walked out the front door.

"Margaret, what are we going to do? This is nobody's fault but Jerry Carter's. Surely, Susanna can see that! She doesn't know everything, especially John's involvement. Please talk to her."

"William, I will, but not now. She's hurting, and if I know my Darlin' she'll come to realize the truth of the matter. Let me wait until tomorrow. By then we'll know if Quincy will make it or not. If the news is good, Susanna will be feelin' better and will be more reasonable. Give her a little time."

"Perhaps you're right. I better go, too. Please call me when you hear anything. Also, sometime tomorrow Bill Maher would like to speak to Susanna. Will you please tell her to contact him?"

"I will do that. Thank you, William, for all your help."

"I wish I could have done more. I'll talk to you tomorrow. Good-bye."

"'Bye, now."

Mrs. O'Hara walked him to the jerry-rigged door and made sure it was closed as securely as she could under the circumstances. On Tuesday she would call and have it repaired or replaced. She turned and walked into the parlor. Picking up the decanter of brandy and two glasses, she walked up the stairs to Susanna's bedroom.

Chapter 31

John Shaw was very upset. After leaving Susanna's house he went to see Detective Maher.

"John, I didn't expect to see you so soon. How's the dog doing?"

"We won't know until tomorrow. If he makes it through the night, his chances of survival are highly increased. Can you tell me the status of Jerry Carter?"

"He's in the hospital under guard. You gave him a good conk on the head. I understand he's conscious but has a concussion. The doctor believes he can be released within twenty-four to forty-eight hours. They want to observe him closely. Once he's medically discharged he will be brought to the county jail and placed in lock-up. He'll be charged with, among other things, breaking and entering, burglary, illegal use of a firearm, and assault. That's just to start with. We will also be charging him with animal endangerment. This charge could be changed depending on what happens."

"Is there any way I can see him?"

"Why would you want to do that?"

"I feel responsible for what happened. Jerry Carter and I were friends for a long time. I just want to ask him, 'Why'?"

"I can't do it in the hospital, but I can try to arrange something when he's in lock-up. I don't want any problems. Make sure that's all you want to ask him. I'll let you know when you can see him. By the way, thank you for the surveillance on the house.

"Your father's pretty smart. He thought Carter might come after the letters again. I know he called you to come back. I talked to him and he told me what he arranged with you. You probably saved that young lady's life."

"I'm afraid it wasn't enough. Thanks for your help, Detective Maher."

Chapter 32

It was a long, restless night for Susanna. The brandy Mrs. O'Hara gave her didn't help. All she could think about was Quincy and what she would do if he didn't survive. He was the only family she had. People might think she was silly for feeling this way, but she couldn't help it, it was the truth.

"Will this night ever end?" she cried out loud.

By six o'clock, she had to get up from bed and move around. Putting on her robe, she heard noises from the kitchen and realized that Mrs. O'Hara was already up. She went down to the kitchen for the telephone call that would eventually come.

"Good morning, Darlin', how are you?"

"I'll be all right. I just wish we would hear from the vet."

"Susanna, it's good that you haven't. It means he made it through the night. I felt he would. Quincy has always been strong and healthy. He has a brave and courageous heart."

"Perhaps you're right but, Mrs. O'Hara, what will I do without him if you're wrong?"

"Give it time. Now, have some coffee and let me make you some breakfast."

As they were eating, or at least trying to eat, the telephone rang, startling both of them. Susanna ran to pick it up.

"Hello!" she said quickly.

"Ms. Smith?"

"Yes!"

"This is Dr. Marlow. I wanted to let you know that Quincy made it through the night. He's still very weak, and his vital signs are not where I want them to be yet, but if he continues to improve like he's doing, he'll make it. He had a rough night. I have to tell you, he's a tough dog."

"Can I see him?"

"Yes, it might do him some good. Why don't you come over around ten and you can see how he is for yourself."

"Thank you so much, Dr. Marlow, I'll see you then."

"Susanna hung up the phone and all the trauma and stress of the last twenty-four hours caught up with her. She looked at Mrs. O'Hara and burst into tears. Mrs. O'Hara got up and hugged her tight.

"Hush, Darlin', the worst is over, he's going to make it. Come sit down," she said calmly.

Chapter 33

At exactly ten o'clock, Susanna and Mrs. O'Hara were ringing the bell at Dr. Marlow's office. Coming to the door, he smiled and let them in.

"I can't believe this dog, what a fighter! I still have him heavily sedated. I don't want him making any jerky moves and re-injuring himself. I'm telling you this so you won't be alarmed and understand why he might not respond. Come on back."

Susanna and Mrs. O'Hara followed him. When they walked into the room, they could see an assortment of cages from tiny to extra large. There were only two other dogs in the room, a dachshund and a basset hound. The former had been spayed and the latter had an injury to his paw. Quincy wasn't in a cage but was on a mat on the floor. He was covered with a lightweight sheet-like cloth. Looking at the mat, Susanna realized it resembled a heating blanket. Then she looked at Quincy and her heart almost stopped. He looked so fragile, so ill. She knelt down next to him on the mat and realized it was keeping him warm. Feeling almost afraid to touch him, that she would hurt him, she held back for a moment.

Dr. Marlow, seeing this, commented, "You can pet him, just be careful of the tubes. Be gentle, it will be all right. But don't stay too long, he needs to rest."

Susanna gently stroked the top of his head and ears.

"Hi, my good and wonderful boy. I'm here. I won't let anybody ever hurt you again," she whispered.

Even sedated, Quincy seemed to know who it was and moved ever so slightly. Susanna continued to pet him and stayed with him for about fifteen minutes. Mrs. O'Hara and Dr. Marlow had left them alone and were waiting outside for her.

"He's very weak. Are you sure he'll be all right?" asked Susanna.

"If he continues to recover like he's doing now he'll be fine. I'm sure you'll be amazed what another twenty-four hours will bring. In fact, you'll probably be able to take him home Thursday or Friday," said Dr. Marlow with authority.

"Would I be able to take him home to New Jersey? Would he be able to travel the five hour trip?"

"Do you have to go home, or can you give him a little more time to heal?"

"I think the sooner I get home the better it will be for everyone," declared Susanna.

"Let's take it a day at a time. By Friday or Saturday he might be able to make the trip. Come back later if you like. Tomorrow I'm open from nine until five. Come in any time. You don't need an appointment. If there's any change, I'll call you right away."

"Thank you for all your help. I'm glad you were here to help Quincy. I'll come back later for a little bit, just so he knows I haven't deserted him. See you later."

Mrs. O'Hara and Susanna left the office and headed back to the house. A meeting was scheduled later in the day with Detective Maher, and, after that, Susanna decided she would come back and spend some time with her faithful companion.

Chapter 34

While Mrs. O'Hara and Susanna were on their way home, John Shaw was sitting in his father's den, talking about the events of the last twenty-four hours.

"John, stop blaming yourself. There was nothing you could have done. You didn't know that Jerry would go over the edge."

"Dad, I just didn't think. You were right. I should never have even suggested him to Susanna. I really thought he had changed, or at least I wanted to believe he had. Look at all the damage he did. I told Bill Maher I wanted to see Jerry."

"Why did you do that? The last person you should see is Jerry Carter!"

"I have to know how he could betray our friendship and do so much harm. I called Dr. Marlow this morning. He told me Quincy made it through the night. He says he's going to make it, Dad. At least I won't have that poor soul's death on my conscience. I don't think Susanna will ever forgive me."

"John, listen to me. She will forgive you once she finds out that you were watching out for her, that you were sitting outside her house making sure she was safe. If you hadn't been there, Jerry might have killed us all. You have to give her time to get over Quincy and the shock of everything that's happened."

"Dad, I know I only met Susanna a little over a week ago, but I really like her and would like to have known her better. I really felt we could have been great together, but I don't think that will happen now. I need to at least make sure that the culprit who caused all this misery goes away for a long time.

"Dad, I'm going over to the vet's to see Quincy."

"I'm going to talk to Mrs. O'Hara later. I'll see how things are. Now that Quincy is out of danger, perhaps she can talk some sense into Susanna. Maybe I can arrange a meeting for the two of you."

"I'd leave it alone, Dad. I'll talk to you later."

William Shaw watched his son leave and a feeling of sadness overcame him. He knew that he had to do something. Surely, he and Margaret could find a way to repair this rift. "I'll call her later and we'll put our heads together," he thought.

Chapter 35

The rest of Memorial Day passed uneventfully for Mrs. O'Hara and Susanna. They went to the police station and reported the events of the day before. They then ate a late lunch and went back to see Quincy who, Susanna believed, looked better. They were back home, having their coffee after dinner.

"I'm sorry I ever came to Weymouth. I should have listened to you. If I had, Quincy wouldn't be hurt. I'm sorry I inherited those letters. They're the root of all the trouble. It's all been about the letters, Mrs. O'Hara."

"Susanna, I'm surprised at you. You have never been one to feel sorry for yourself. You've always accepted responsibility and did what had to be done. The letters, this trip, all of it brought you closer to your family. This is a good thing. I know you don't want to hear this, but good always comes out of bad. You'll see. This happened for a reason."

"What could be the reason for hurting Quincy? No, when he's better I'm taking him home. I'm going to sell this place and everything in it and put this all behind me."

"Susanna, running away from everything will not solve nor settle anything. You have to face it all head on and then make your decision. You need to finish the letters and have closure on your family. Only then can you put this behind you," she said.

Susanna saw the determined look on Mrs. O'Hara's face and realized what she said had some merit. "Maybe I'm wrong. Maybe I'm still too upset to think rationally," she thought. Then she made a plan.

"Mrs. O'Hara, you may be right. I'm probably not in any shape to make any major decisions. I'm going to finish the letters tonight, and before we go home to New Jersey I will make a decision about the house. If possible, I'll go to the Adams Homestead. That might help fill in the gaps. I'll give it some time and then decide."

"Darlin', that's the girl I know and love! Now, let's talk about John Shaw."

"No, I don't want to talk about him or see him again. I'm going upstairs to read the letters then get some sleep. I need to see Quincy early in the morning, and then go see Mary at the library and tell her what happened. Thank you for everything Mrs. O'Hara. I don't know how I would have handled this without you. You've been wonderful."

Susanna went over and hugged her tight, then went upstairs.

Watching her leave the kitchen, Mrs. O'Hara knew that this was not the end of their discussion. She also knew that Susanna liked John Shaw. "How can I show her? 'Tis a pity she's not aware of his involvement. Somehow I have to get the two of them together." The ringing telephone brought her out of her thoughts.

"Margaret, it's William. Can you talk?"

Chapter 36

Dearest Friend   *Braintree August 10 1775*

Tis with a sad Heart I take my pen to write to you because I must be the bearer of what will greatly afflict and distress you. Yet I wish you to be prepaired for the Event. Your Brother Elihu lies very dangerously sick with Dysentery. He has been very bad for more than a week, his life is despaired of. Er'e I close this Letter I fear I shall write you that he is no more.

We are all in great distress. Your Mother is with him in great anguish. I hear this morning that he is sensible of his Danger, and calmly resigned to the will of Heaven: which is great Satisfaction to his mourning Friend's. I cannot write more at present than to assure you of the Health of your own family. Mr. Elisha Niles lies very bad with the same disorder.—*Adieu* (24)

August 11

I have this morning occasion to sing of Mercies and judgments. May I properly notice each—a mixture of joy and grief agitate my Bosom. The return of thee my dear partner after a four months absence is a pleasure I cannot express, but the joy is overclouded, and the Day is darkened by the mixture of Grief and the Sympathy I feel for the loss of your Brother, cut of in the pride of life and the bloom of Manhood! In the midst of his usefulness; Heaven san[c]tify this affliction to us, and make me properly thankful that it is not my sad lot to mourn the loss of a Husband in the room of a Brother. May thy life be spaired and thy Health confirmed for the benefit of thy Country and the happiness of thy family is the constant supplication of thy Friend (25)

Dearest Friend   *Braintree Sepbr. 25 1775*

I set down with a heavy Heart to write to you. I have had no other since you left me. Woe follows Woe and one affliction treads upon the heal of an other. My distress for my own family having in some measure abated; tis excited anew upon the distress of my dear Mother. Her kindness brought her to see me every day when I was ill and our little Tommy. She has taken the disorder and lies so bad that we have little hopes of her Recovery. She is possess'd with the Idea that she shall not recover, and I fear it will prove but too true.

In this Town the distemper seems to have abated. We have none now so bad as Patty. She has lain 21 days, each day we had reason to think would be her last, but [a] good Constitution, and youth for ought I know will finally *conquer the distemper. She is not able to get out of Bed, nor can she help herself any more than a new born infant. Yet there are symptoms which now appear in her favour.*

The desolation of War is not so distressing as the Havock made by the pestilence. Some poor parents are mourning the loss of 3, 4, and 5 children, and some families are wholy striped of every Member.

Wherefore is it that we are thus contended with? How much reason have I for thankfulness that all my family are spaired whilst so many others are striped of their parents, their children, their husbands.

O kind Heaven spair my parents, spair my Dearest Friend and grant him Health. Continue the lives and health of our dear children. Sister Elihu Adams lost her youngest child last night with this disorder. I can add no more than Supplications for your welfare, and an ardent desire to hear from you by every opportunity. It will alleviate every trouble thro which it may be my Lot to pass. I am most affectionately your distress'd (26)

Portia

Weymouth october. 1 1775

Have pitty upon me, have pitty upon me o! thou my beloved for the Hand of God presseth me soar. Yet will I be dumb and silent and not open my mouth becaus thou o Lord hast done it.

How can I tell you (o my bursting Heart) that my Dear Mother has Left me, this day about 5 oclock she left this world for an infinitely better.

After sustaining 16 days severe conflict nature fainted and she fell asleep. Blessed Spirit where art thou?

At times I almost am ready to faint under this severe and heavy Stroke, seperated from thee who used to be a comfortar towards me in affliction, but blessed be God, his Ear is not heavy that he cannot hear, but he has bid us call upon him in time of Trouble.

I know you are a sincere and hearty mourner with me and will pray for me in my affliction. My poor father like a firm Believer and a Good christian sets before his children the best of Examples of patience and submission. My sisters send their Love to you and are greatly afflicted.

You often Express'd your anxiety for me when you left me before, surrounded with Terrors, but my trouble then was as the small dust in the balance compaird to what I have since endured. I hope to be properly mindful of the correcting hand, that I may not be rebuked in anger.—You will pardon and forgive all my wanderings of mind. I cannot be correct.

'Tis a dreadful time with this whole province. Sickness and death are in almost every family. I have no more shocking and terrible Idea of any Distemper except the Plague than this.

Almighty God restrain the pestilence which walketh in darkeness and wasteth at noon day and which has laid in the dust one of the dearest of parents. May the Life of the other be lenghtend out to his afflicted children and Your distressd (27)

Portia

The wooden box of letters was lying along the side of the bed on the floor. Susanna had read all but one of the letters. This one letter was still in the box and was lengthy. She would read it tonight and finish the saga of Abigail. While she believed the letters were the cause of all her present day woes, she still didn't want them to end. The letters were a link to her family and history. From their content she discovered that Abigail and she had much in common. There was no denying the importance of these letters. Looking to Quincy's empty pillow, she realized how much she missed him and how much she talked to him. She hoped he was doing better and would go to see him early tomorrow. Susanna had to go to the library, as well, to see Mary and return the book she had borrowed. She hadn't had a chance to read it with everything going on. Holding it in her, hands she thought about the letters again.

It was such a trying time in American history and in Abigail Adams life. "Maybe I should go through the book before I return it. It might fill in the rest of the blanks," she thought. "If Mary has time tomorrow, perhaps we can talk about Abigail. I should also talk to Mr. Shaw. He's been so helpful, so protective. He needs to know I don't hold him responsible for any of this."

"Oh Quincy, I really miss you," she cried.

November 27 1775

Tis a fortnight to Night since I wrote you a line during which, I have been confined with the Jaundice, Rhumatism and a most voilent cold; I yesterday took a puke which has releived me, and I feel much better to day. Many, very many people who have had the dysentery, are now afflicted both with the Jaundice and Rhumatisim, some it has left in Hecticks, some in dropsies.

The great and incessant rains we have had this fall, (the like cannot be recollected) may have occasiond some of the present disorders. The Jaundice is very prevelant in the

Camp. We have lately had a week of very cold weather, as cold as January, and a flight of snow, which I hope will purify the air of some of the noxious vapours. It has spoild many hundreds of Bushels of Apples, which were designd for cider, and which the great rains had prevented people from making up. Suppose we have lost 5 Barrels by it.

Col. Warren returnd last week to Plymouth, so that I shall not hear any thing from you till he goes back again which will not be till the last of (next) this month.

He Damp'd my Spirits greatly by telling me that the Court had prolonged your Stay an other month. I was pleasing myself with the thoughts that you would soon be upon your return. Tis in vain to repine. I hope the publick will reap what I sacrifice.

I wish I knew what mighty things were fabricating. If a form of Government is to be established here what one will be assumed? Will it be left to our assemblies to chuse one? and will not many men have many minds? and shall we not run into Dissentions among ourselves?

I am more and more convinced that Man is a dangerous creature, and that power whether vested in many or a few is ever grasping, and like the grave cries give, give. The great fish swallow up the small, and he who is most strenuous for the Rights of the people, when vested with power, is as eager after the perogatives of Government. You tell me of degrees of perfection to which Humane Nature is capable of arriving, and I believe it, but at the same time lament that our admiration should arise from the scarcity of the instances.

The Building up a Great Empire, which was only hinted at by my correspondent may now I suppose be realized even by the unbelievers. Yet will not ten thousand Difficulties arise in the formation of it? The Reigns of Government have been so long slakned, that I fear the people will not quietly submit to those restraints which are necessary for the peace, and security, of the community: if we seperate from Brittain, what Code of Laws will be established. How shall we be governd so as to retain our Liberties? Can any government be free which is not adminstred by general stated Laws? Who shall frame these Laws? Who will give them force and energy? Tis true your Resolution[s] as a Body have heithertoo had the force of Laws. But will they continue to have?

When I consider these things and the prejudices of people in favour of Ancient customs and Regulations, I feel anxious for the fate of our Monarchy or Democracy or what ever is to take place. I soon get lost in a Labyrinth of perplexities, but whatever occurs, may justice and righteousness be the Stability of our times, and order arise out of confusion. Great difficulties may be surmounted, by patience and perserverance.

I believe I have tired you with politicks. As to news we have not any at all. I shudder at the approach of winter when I think I am to remain desolate. Suppose your weather is warm yet. Mr. Mason and Thaxter live with me, and render some part of my time less disconsolate. Mr. Mason is a youth who will please you, he has Spirit, taste and Sense. His application to his Studies is constant and I am much mistaken if he does not make a very good figure in his profession.

I have with me now, the only Daughter of your Brother; I feel a tenderer affection for her as she has lost a kind parent. Though too young to be sensible of her own loss, I can pitty her. She appears to be a child of a very good Disposition—only wants to be a little used to company.

I have settld the matter of Josiah Quincy. Due to such sensitive natures I have not been able to write of the matter, but can now: it was murder most Foul. As I suspectd. Dr. Smyth and Major Mifflin helpd me set the trap. Major Mifflin carred out your orders to assist me. Tis only four days past, but done. Mr. Page has been removd from Tory support and the secret papers saved; back in the right hands. O my Dearest, Mr. Quincy was poisond; cut down before his time. Your friend and mentor, Mr. Page will be punishd. I have the prof and Mr. Quincy will rest in peace. Dr. Smythe and Major Mifflin waitd for him in his room and surprisd him. They found the papers and put them in a safe place. The matter is settld. I hope you are proud of me for that wich I have done. I will meet with the widow Quincy and tell her all when I am recoverd. You may wish to burn this letter after reading for safty. (I)*

Our Little ones send Duty to pappa and want much to see him. Tom says he wont come home till the Battle is over—some strange notion he has got in his head. He has got a political cread to say to him when he returns.

*(I) *See Chapter Notes.*

Dear John

I must bid you good night. 'Tis late for one who am much of an invalide. I was disappointed last week in receiving a packet by the post, and upon unsealing it found only four news papers. I think you are more cautious than you need be. All Letters I believe have come safe to hand. I have Sixteen from you, and wish I had as many more. Adieu. Yours (28)

Chapter 37

Susanna left the house around nine in the morning. Mrs. O'Hara stayed home to wait for the carpenter, who was going to fix the front door, and a locksmith.

Checking on Quincy was top priority for Susanna, and she was happy to see him so improved. He knew she was there and he even wagged his little stub. Dr. Marlow said he was doing very well and that she could come to get him Friday morning. Telling Dr. Marlow that she would come back later in the afternoon, she left to go to the library and speak with Mary.

Mary Connors was sitting behind the front desk as Susanna came into the library. As she looked up from her books, she smiled when she saw who was standing there.

"Susanna. Hi! How was your weekend?" she asked.

"It was exciting to say the least. I want to return the book I borrowed Friday. I was also wondering if you would have any time to talk. I need to tell you what happened and to explain what I'm going to do."

"Sounds serious. Can you give me a few minutes to get someone to cover the front desk? Then we can go back to my office."

Dear John

"Great, I'll wait right here."

Sitting in Mary's office brought back memories of when she used to visit Aunt Susanna. Very little had changed.

"So, what's going on?" asked Mary.

Susanna quickly related the events since Friday night. She omitted nothing, not even her outrage at John Shaw. When she was done, Mary came over and hugged her.

"How's Quincy? How are you?"

"I'll be all right and fortunately so will Quincy. He needs time to heal, but the vet assures me he will be his old self again, soon."

"That's wonderful news. I have to meet Mrs. O'Hara—she sounds like a gem!"

"She is. I don't know what I would have done without her."

"What will you do now?" asked Mary.

"This brings me to my next reason for coming. After reading the old letters, I realized how fortunate I am for being related to Abigail Adams. I come from a long line of strong women, my aunt being one of them. These letters just reaffirmed everything."

"What's in them Susanna? Why don't you tell me about them?"

"They're a story about life, love, war, anguish, sadness, mystery and, most important, a remarkable marriage. Do you have time to hear about them?"

Nodding her head, Mary got up to get both of them a cup of tea. After she handed Susanna a cup, she sat down and waited for her to begin.

"The letters begin in May 1775, shortly after the Battle of Lexington and Concord and right after John Adams had left to sit in the Second Continental Congress. John had been home in Boston with Abigail and the family from October 1774 until April 1775. During this six-month interval at home, many things changed on the political front. In fact, it was very eventful. John returned to a Congress that had shifted dramatically, and he had left behind a wife and family in uncertain times. (29)

"Blood had spilled during this first battle. The former Governor of Massachusetts, whose name was Hutchinson, had his house ransacked. Letters were found and published in the Boston newspaper, that many felt were incriminating. Boston also witnessed the new Governor, Commander Gage, along with his military forces, under siege by the colonials. It was a hotbed of intrigue. Houses were abandoned, including John's and Abigail's, to the British military and loyalists. People who were trusted friends and neighbors were now spying for or informing to the British. Not knowing who to turn to, the inhabitants from the town left in droves and went to the countryside to find refuge. Bostonians were literally looking for a safe haven."(30)

"Mary, can't you just imagine it! How strong she must have been, resilient as well. Living at this time and in this country, everything so unsettled and at war. There are people fleeing Boston, and your husband is miles away. Your home in Boson is taken over by the British and you can't get to it. You're left behind to manage your farm in Braintree—and the family—not knowing if the British will attack or if you will even live! Your husband, having the faith and trust in your business acumen, knowing that you will do the right thing."

"Susanna, please go on."

"Here is another interesting thing to come out of the letters. The actual conflict came to Braintree when the British raided a place called Grape Island, the purpose being to get hay to feed their horses. John's two brothers were among the many who fought back. Braintree began to fill up with refugees and local people, including Abigail, took them into their homes. Some even took over houses that had been abandoned by the Loyalists. One of these houses was the Vassall-Borland place.

"What's so interesting about all of this, but maybe you already know, is that this was the future home of four generations of the Adams family. It's what's now known as the Adams Homestead."(31)

"I didn't know that. I visited there a few years ago when I was in high school. I'm afraid back then I didn't pay attention to such details," said Mary.

"I was supposed to go there, if you remember, with Mr. Shaw on Saturday. With everything that happened, we never made it. I really need to see it, but I'm not sure I'll make it there before I go home. It all depends upon Quincy."

"You still have some time left. Maybe you'll get there. Please, continue."

"Mary, during this period and for some time after, it was difficult to send or receive mail. British Loyalists or military intercepted letters. Both John and Abigail had to be careful. John had two of his letters intercepted, one to Abigail and the other to his friend James Warren. In the letters, John, who was at the Second Continental Congress, voiced his impatience with the impasse of the Congress. He especially mentioned John Dickinson of Pennsylvania who was trying to establish a compromise with Great Britain. These letters, after interception, were published in Tory newspapers.

"It created a problem for John, but eventually the notoriety calmed down. What this situation did result in, however, was that they ensured that any letters or correspondence was delivered in a very cautious manner. (32)

"This type of arrangement frustrated Abigail. John worried about the letters and was very circumspect in what he wrote. What I discovered in Abigail's letters was a frustration at not hearing from John. She would often rebuke him about not receiving anything. Left alone with the war all around her, weary, she looked to these letters for reassurance. Mary, there was also a mystery and murder that Abigail actually helped to solve."

"You're kidding me! A murder? Who? What happened?"

"There was a friend of John's by the name of Josiah Quincy who died mysteriously right after John had left for the Second Congress. Abigail wrote and told John that there was something not right about his passing and that she was going to check into it. She talked to Josiah's widow and, more importantly, to his doctor. The doctor believed Josiah was poisoned for some secret documents that he had in his possession. Prior to his death, Quincy was visited twice by an Englishman whose name was Page. It turned out that this Englishman poisoned Josiah Quincy and took the secret documents. He was protected in Boston by the military and was practically untouchable.

"Abigail wrote to John about all this but was worried the letters might be intercepted. John also worried and had a plan carried back to Braintree and to Abigail in the person of a Major Miflin. They met and hatched a plan to capture Mr. Page and retrieve the documents. Abigail, Dr. Smythe and Major Miflin set a trap for Mr. Page. With the help of some others, they found Page in his lodgings. This murderer was captured and the papers put back into safe hands."

"Amazing! She arranged all this and helped to bring this man to justice. Susanna, she sounds like quite a lady. These letters make her seem so real—not like what we learned in history class," said Mary.

"Mary, there's more. You should read how she took care of the farm. She even had a run in with one of her tenants, a stubborn New Englander who refused to share part of the rented house to a family fleeing Boston. Abigail was furious. She had to write to John and asked him to please write to the tenant and tell him he had to share the space, as he wouldn't listen to Abigail or do what she asked.

"When I read this letter, I thought to myself times haven't changed. I remembered an incident I had with an insurance company last year. I had a problem with the policy. I knew what was wrong, but I had the guy on the other end of the telephone have the nerve to ask me if there was a man he could explain it to. That way, the man could explain it to me so I would understand what the difficulty was! I'm glad this happened over the telephone, because if this person were near me, I'd have gone for his jugular.

"I really understood Abigail's frustration. The actual running of the farm had been left up to her. It was a lot of responsibility. John couldn't do it. He was miles away in Philadelphia, helping to create a new nation. The only one she could really rely on was herself. He knew she could do it. She was his equal in their marriage and in business.

"If you really look at the women of the times, they had to shoulder this type of responsibility. They worked side by side with their husbands before the War. When the War actually started, they took their husbands' place at home while the husbands fought or helped form a new government. Mary, this type of equality between the sexes got buried in later years and didn't reappear until World War II. We, as women, should thank these ladies. They really were the first feminists."

"Such role models! Susanna, would you like another cup of tea? I have cookies as well if you would like some."

"Thanks, I would."

Mary got up from her chair, refilled Susanna's cup and brought out a bag of shortbread cookies for them both. When they were settled again, Susanna told Mary more of what was in the letters.

"It was amazing to me how much illness was around at this time. John came home for a short time in August and early September during a recess. After he left to go back to Philadelphia, Abigail and most of the family became ill with a very deadly strain of dysentery. This soon became an epidemic. In the process, Abigail lost her mother, and John lost his brother Elihu and Elihu's daughter to the disease. Abigail was beside herself with grief. Her strength came from her strong religious convictions and belief that her mother and John's family were in a better place. (33)

"The last letter in the series was probably the most endearing one to me. It was written in November of 1775. Abigail was ill again, claiming she had jaundice, rheumatism and a very bad cold. Sitting up late the night she wrote the letter, she speaks of "incessant rains," the spoilage of apples, and the cold weather. Mundane items, but they show a concern for the farm and the hardships that occurred.

"She then goes on to talk about the formation of the new government. She voices her concerns about how it will be established and the difficulties involved in this formation. She speaks so passionately and with such intelligence about these political matters that one forgets her lack of a formal education. Her intuitive knowledge about people and society in general shows a wisdom about human nature that is unparalleled. (34)

"Mary, I've grown to really like her! I'm so proud to be her descendent. I'm also proud to have had such a wonderful aunt. Even with all that has happened because of these letters, I now know why my Aunt Susanna left them to me. She brought me back to my family and made me realize how important family is. I'm only sorry I realized this so late. I need to make both my aunt and Abigail proud of me. I will have to make something of my life that is more important than my own needs."

"What will you do now Susanna? I hope you keep the house. We've just met and I would hate to see our friendship end. Please tell me you're doing that."

"I don't know for sure what I'm going to do, but I will tell you this: no matter where I live, we will still be friends. I will make a point to see you and to get together often."

Mary got up and gave Susanna another hug. They walked to the door together. Before she left the library, Susanna promised that they would get together for dinner. She also promised to bring Mrs. O'Hara. They wouldn't go back to New Jersey without saying goodbye.

"I'll call you later to set up when and where we'll meet for dinner. Take care, Mary, and thanks for listening."

"Susanna, give Quincy a hug for me. I look forward to meeting Mrs. O'Hara. Bye-bye."

Susanna left the library and went back to the vet to spend some time with Quincy. It had been another tiring day.

Chapter 38

Susanna noticed the new front door right away. She also noticed the shiny new lock. "Leave it to Mrs. O'Hara," she thought. She walked into the house and the aroma of lamb roasting wafted toward her. Her taste buds were immediately tantalized. Susanna realized how hungry she was. She never had lunch after seeing Mary. Instead, she had gone to visit Quincy and spent the afternoon with him. Going into the kitchen, she saw Mrs. O'Hara stirring a pot on the stove and quietly singing to herself.

"Wow! Something smells delicious."

"Hello, Darlin'. I thought we needed a good hearty meal. How's my little lad doing?" she asked.

"He was alert—actually moved around a little. He's still weak, but he sat next to me and put his head in my lap. They told me he ate a little today and drank some water. Dr. Marlow says he's doing very well considering the nature of his injuries and that I should be able to take him home Friday morning."

"That's grand, Darlin'! I need to tell you before we get too much further that I invited William to dinner tonight. He's a good man, and I felt we needed to thank him for all his help. I hope that's all right with you?"

"That's fine Mrs. O'Hara. I actually had decided to call him tonight. I have a few things to talk to him about. When's he coming?"

"He should be here at six."

"Good, that gives me time to change. I smell like a dog. I'll be right back to help you."

"Take your time, everything's under control and just needs finishing up. The table is already set, so don't rush."

Chapter 39

"*John, its Bill Maher. I* just wanted you to know that Jerry Carter is being moved to County Jail tomorrow. The doctor has cleared him and we should be moving him sometime before noon. If you want, I can arrange a meeting for sometime on Friday. I can't do it tomorrow or Thursday, too much processing to be done. Do you want me to make the arrangements?" he asked.

"Thanks, I would. What time?"

"I'll set it up for ten and meet you there to walk you through. I hear his bookies aren't happy with him either. He's safer in jail than on the street. You should also know that we found the fence he used in Boston. We were able to locate everything on the inventory list except the silver tea set. He must have used a collector for that particular piece. We may never find it. When you talk to him, see if he'll tell you where it is. He won't tell us. I'm going to stop by and see Miss Smith tomorrow and tell her."

"That's good news, Detective. It's a shame about the tea set, but I'll see if there's anything I can find out about it."

"How's the dog doing?'

"I stopped by the vet this morning and he's going to recover. Dr. Marlow said he's one lucky dog. I think once he's feeling better, he's going to lap up all this attention. Quincy's really a great dog. He even likes me! More than what I can say for his owner."

"I think once she finds out what you did for her and how you tried to prevent all this, she'll turn around."

"I guess time will tell. I'll see you on Friday."

Chapter 40

William Shaw arrived promptly at six. He brought with him an expensive bottle of merlot wine for dinner and Bailey's Irish Cream for afterwards. He gave Mrs. O'Hara a peck on the cheek and followed her to the kitchen. Susanna hadn't come down yet, and he took this opportunity to speak to Mrs. O'Hara.

"How's she doing?" he said quietly.

"Better today. The lad's doing well and she saw Mary today. I think this perked her up quite a bit."

"Good, I'm glad. I was very worried about her. I'm hoping we can both make her realize that John shouldn't be held responsible for this travesty. He tried so hard to protect her."

Before she could reply, Susanna walked into the kitchen.

"Hi, Mr. Shaw! Doesn't it smell great in here? I'm starving, Mrs. O'Hara. When can we eat?"

"We can eat in five minutes. William, why don't you open that lovely bottle of wine? I would love to have a wee taste."

"My pleasure!" he smiled as he opened the bottle.

Mrs. O'Hara had outdone herself. In spite of the circumstances, dinner was enjoyable, comforting and delicious. They spoke about everything but what had happened recently.

After dessert, Mrs. O'Hara told Susanna and William to go into the parlor and that she would join them shortly. She really wanted William to have some time alone with Susanna.

"Fix some glasses of Bailey's and take them with you, William. I'll have mine over ice, if you will. I'll be right there," said Mrs. O'Hara.

William and Susanna went into the parlor and sat down. William Shaw looked around the room and became nostalgic. There were so many good memories from this house. What happened over the weekend had cast a cloud on these memories. He thought how upset his Susanna would have felt about those events.

"Susanna, how are you really?" he asked.

"I'm better today. Quincy's improving and I'll be able to take him home soon."

"So, you're going to leave us?"

"Yes, I'm going to take Quincy back to New Jersey where he can recuperate in familiar surroundings. I think Mrs. O'Hara and I need to go home as well. A lot has happened and I really need to get my routine back. I need structure again. I have to put this all behind me."

"What will you do with the house?" he inquired.

"I wanted to talk to you about that. I talked with Mrs. O'Hara the other night and she made me realize that I shouldn't make any rash decisions. So, I was wondering if I could ask you to take care of things up here for me until I can make those decisions. The house needs to be cared for. It will need some upkeep. I can set up an account with you so that you could pay whoever does the work."

"I will be happy to do anything I can to help you. However, you need to know I will miss you. I've only known you a short time, but I've grown very fond of you. You remind me so much of your aunt. You have so many of her qualities. She would be so proud of you and the way you have handled yourself."

"Thank you. That's the nicest thing you could have said. Since I've been here, I've realized how much I miss her, and my parents, too. Sometimes I wish I could go back in time and change things. I would especially have spent more time with her. Do you think I'm being foolish?"

"No, I wish I could have those years back as well. I miss your aunt very much. I loved her deeply, and I think she loved me as well. But, you can't have time back. You have to go on and live your life. She would want you to do this."

"I need time, but I can tell you this: Weymouth and this house have a strong emotional tie for me."

"Susanna, I need to talk to you about John and what has happened."

"Please Mr. Shaw. I don't want to go into this with you."

At this moment Mrs. O'Hara came in from the kitchen. She had overheard their conversation and wanted to intervene.

"William, the Bailey's is grand!"

"Margaret, I was just telling Susanna I needed to speak to her about John and his involvement in this affair. I think she needs to know what he did. Don't you agree?"

"What do you mean what he did? I know what he did! He brought a horrible person into my home!" cried Susanna.

"Darlin', stop it. You are looking for someone to blame for Quincy's injuries. 'Tis only Jerry Carter who is responsible. In fact, John had no control over what happened. He actually kept you from being injured and possibly killed."

"I don't understand, what do you mean?" asked Susanna.

"Susanna, after the break-in I called John and told him what happened. I was unhappy with you staying here and he agreed. Detective Maher also called him. We both felt he could take up the surveillance of you and the house between police patrols. He was outside your house from Saturday night until

Jerry broke in. He will never forgive himself for not realizing the depth of desperation on Jerry's part. John never felt he was dangerous or that he would have a gun. Had he known, he would have stopped him before the attack. Maher needed proof that Jerry was the one who was responsible."

"He told me he had Jerry Carter's fingerprints," said Susanna.

"Which was true. However, Jerry had been in the house the day before. You had given him permission to be there. It was logical that his fingerprints would also be there. Had this gone to court, a good lawyer would have gotten him off. The police needed more in order to get a conviction. That was why John waited for him to break in again."

"Darlin', listen to what William is saying. Jerry Carter is the hooligan here."

"This may all be true, but John brought him here. He's known him since college, and he knew he had been in trouble before. He should never have trusted him."

"Susanna, they were friends. Haven't you ever had a friend who was in trouble and you helped? Someone you wanted to believe had changed and were willing to give a second chance?" said William.

"I have friends, but none who would have done this!"

"Susanna, I told you before that you had many qualities of your aunt, but I can see forgiveness is not one of them. She would have understood. I think I've said all that I can. Please let me know your plans and drop off the keys to the house before you leave Weymouth. I promise to take care of things for you until you decide what to do. Goodnight, Susanna. Margaret, thank you for a lovely dinner. I will speak to you before you go home. Good bye."

William Shaw got up and left the house. Susanna watched him go and was crushed. He had hit home. She thought that maybe she was being unreasonable, but it still hurt. Quincy had been her only family for the last five years and the thought that she could have lost him forever was still causing her anguish.

"Darlin,' I have never known you to be so hard. This young man needs to be heard."

Mrs. O'Hara looked at Susanna and shook her head. She only had a couple of days to prove to her that John should be given a second chance. He was the right man for Susanna. She was just too bull-headed to realize it.

"Darlin', at least think about it. I think we're both tired. Things will look better in the morning. Let's go to bed."

Chapter 41

John Shaw pulled into the driveway of Susanna's house. Cautiously getting out of the car, he wondered if he should attempt to talk to Susanna.

As he looked, he realized her car wasn't even there.

"I bet she's not home. I'll come back later," he said out loud.

As he was getting back into his car, the front door opened and Mrs. O'Hara called to him.

"John, please don't go."

"Mrs. O'Hara, I didn't think anyone was at home. I didn't see Susanna's car. Is she here?"

"No, she's with Quincy. Please, come in and have a cup of coffee with me."

"I'm not sure that's a good idea. Susanna made it clear she doesn't want me around."

"Don't be silly, I want you to come in. I need to talk to you. Please, I made some scones!"

"Thank you, I would like that."

Sitting at the kitchen nook, Mrs. O'Hara saw a weary John Shaw. She thought to herself that this had taken as big a toll on John as it did on Susanna. She poured him a cup of coffee and put out the scones with jam and cream.

"John, please help yourself."

"Thank you. They look delicious."

"John, I'm sorry about all that's happened. You need to know I don't hold you responsible. In fact, I want to thank you for watching out for Susanna and myself over the weekend. Lord knows what might have happened if you weren't out there."

"It was the least I could do. I never thought anyone would get hurt. I came here today to try and talk to Susanna and ask her to forgive me for putting you all in such danger. I'm sorry I missed her," he said sadly.

"John, she'll come around. Give her some time. She needs to get over the shock of Quincy. She's going to take him back to New Jersey to heal, but she hasn't given up on Weymouth. Her roots go too deep."

"When are you leaving?" he asked

"It all depends on Quincy and the vet, but I think it will be Friday. We talked this morning and between today and tomorrow we will get ready to close up the house. We also plan on meeting Mary Connors for dinner Thursday night at the Ivy Inn. I think Susanna said six o'clock. Just in case you're interested."

"Thanks again, Mrs. O'Hara for the information and the scones. I have to go, I'll talk to you before you go home." He gave her a kiss on the cheek and went on his way.

She watched him leave and thought to herself that she had done everything she could to heal the rift between them. It was up to the two of them now.

"I better get busy, I have a lot to do before Friday," she thought.

Chapter 42

Wednesday and Thursday passed without incident. Susanna and Mrs. O'Hara cleaned and prepared to close up the house. As Susanna was packing her suitcase, the telephone rang.

"Ms. Smith?"

"Hi, Detective Maher, how are things going?"

"I wanted to let you know that Jerry Carter was moved to County Jail yesterday. He was arraigned today. His bail was set high and I never thought he would meet the rate. But it seems somebody came in and paid it for him. I wanted you to know he is out. I will have cars patrolling just in case. We also located almost all of the items on your inventory list. Unfortunately, we didn't find the tea set. We'll still keep looking. Maybe it will turn up. When are you going back to New Jersey?"

"Tomorrow morning. I'll pick up Quincy and then take him home. Mrs. O'Hara will also be leaving tomorrow. Detective Maher, will he come after us?"

"I don't think so. I believe Jerry has other things to worry about. Where will you be tonight?"

"We're going to meet Mary Connors at the Ivy Inn, then come home to finish packing."

"I'll keep a watch on the house. You'll need to come back to testify at the trial. I have your address and telephone number in New Jersey and will keep you informed as to what's going on. Have a safe trip home. Take care of that beautiful dog."

"Thanks for your help, Detective Maher."

Susanna hung up the phone and wondered if she should be worried. Surely, Jerry Carter would keep a low profile. Looking at her watch, Susanna saw that she needed to hurry. It was five-thirty. They had to get going.

Chapter 43

"Darlin', what a charming place. It reminds me so of Ireland. The cottage, the ivy, the garden—brings back so many memories of my childhood."

"Wait until you see the inside. It's really quaint. Oh look! There's Mary. We timed this just right. Let's go, Mrs. O'Hara."

Mary Connors had pulled into the parking lot of the Ivy Inn right after Susanna and Mrs. O'Hara. She saw them getting out of the car and thought how much Mrs. O'Hara looked exactly like she had pictured her.

"Hi, Mary!"

"Hello! This must be Mrs. O'Hara. It's so nice to meet you at last. I've heard so much about you."

"Mary! 'Tis nice to meet you, too!"

They all went inside and sat down for dinner. The dining room was filling up and there were only three tables left.

After being seated close to the table that she had shared with John, Susanna suddenly felt sad. The fireplace was crackling, as it had been before, and the flowers on the tables were fresh cut and colorful.

Facing the front of the dining room, Susanna could see everyone who came into the restaurant. As she looked up from her menu, she was startled to see John Shaw standing there. He was headed for their table!

"Mrs. O'Hara! Mary! Susanna! What a nice surprise. How are you all doing? Susanna, how's Quincy?"

Before she could answer, John's cell phone rang.

"Hi, Dad! What's going on?"

The expression on John's face changed drastically. He shut the phone off and looked pale. Mrs. O'Hara noticed it right away and got up to steady him.

"John, what's wrong? Is your father all right?"

Sitting down at the table, John looked at all of them and then spoke directly to Susanna.

"Detective Maher called my father and asked him to get in touch with me. He wanted me to know that they found Jerry Carter's body in a back alley in Boston. He was beaten to death, tortured really. Please excuse me. I have to talk to his family. I'm sorry for ruining your dinner. Goodnight."

Before anyone could stop him, John quickly exited the restaurant.

"What a sad end to a life. He may not have been a great lad but he didn't deserve to end up like that. He was someone's son. His mother will be heartsick," said Mrs. O'Hara gently.

Susanna had not spoken a word the entire time. She now looked at Mary and Mrs. O'Hara and began to weep softly. In a little while, she composed herself.

"I didn't like Jerry Carter, but I certainly didn't want this. All of a sudden I'm not very hungry. Would you mind if we cancel dinner?" said Susanna.

"Mary, please come back to the house with us. I'll fix a little something for us to eat, and I think we can all use some brandy. Let's get the waiter and our check," said Mrs. O'Hara.

Chapter 44

After the horrible news at the restaurant, they all went back to Susanna's house. No one had much of an appetite, but Mrs. O'Hara made omelets and gave each girl, including herself, a brandy. They talked of life, love, death and family. Mary, assured that Susanna and Mrs. O'Hara would be all right, promised to keep in touch and said her final goodbyes to both of them around eleven.

"Mrs. O'Hara, I'm so sorry about all of this. I realize now I shouldn't have been so hard on John. He was helping a friend. If it had been you, I would have done the same thing. I really made a royal mess of things. Maybe I can reach him in the morning before I pick up Quincy. I hope so, anyway."

"Darlin', I think that's a good idea John could use some good news right now. But what happens if you can't reach him?"

"I don't know. But I have to try. After I get Quincy, I'll stop by Mr. Shaw's office. I need to drop the keys off and settle everything with him as well. If I can't reach John, maybe he can tell me where he is."

"I think we need to get some rest. Don't stay up too late, Darlin'. Tomorrow will be a busy day," said Mrs. O'Hara.

"I won't. I need to unwind and think things through. Goodnight. See you in the morning."

Susanna stayed in the parlor after Mrs. O'Hara had gone up the stairs to bed. She knew what she had to do. It was the right thing. Sitting at her aunt's desk she took out a piece of paper and began to write. By two o'clock she was finished with her task and was tired enough to go to bed and get some sleep. Standing up, she looked around the parlor for the last time. Her eye glimpsed the photographs that had been put back into frames and placed again on the piano. She walked over and picked up the picture of her aunt.

"Aunt Susanna, you were a sharp cookie. You knew I would come here. You knew I would do the right thing. I hope I haven't disappointed you. Thank you for showing me my family history. Thank you for allowing me to meet Abigail Adams and thank you for showing me such good friends. Most of all, thank you for being my aunt. I hope you never doubted how much I loved you."

Yawning, Susanna went upstairs to bed.

Chapter 45

By nine in the morning John Shaw was entering his father's office. He looked very tired. It had been a long night.

"Holly, is my dad available?"

"Yes he is. Let me tell him you're here."

William Shaw was sitting at his desk when Holly called to tell him John wanted to see him. He got up from his desk to greet his son.

"John, how are Mr. and Mrs. Carter doing?"

"Dad, his mom was destroyed. Detective Maher asked me to identify the body. His parent's were too distraught to do it."

John looked at his dad and broke down. William put his hand on John's shoulder and waited for him to compose himself.

"Dad, you should have seen him. How could anybody do that? It was brutal. I had to check for his tattoo to make sure it really was him. No matter what he did he didn't deserve this. Bill Maher believes it was his bookie. He owed a great deal of money. He also believes it was the bookie who bailed him out. He said that the murder is under investigation, but he doesn't hold much hope of a conviction."

"John, go home and get some rest, it's been a difficult time for you. I'll certainly do what I can for the family. Do you know when they'll release the body to the family?"

"I don't know Dad, but I promised Jerry's mom that I would come back and help her with the funeral plans. I'm going to go home to clean up and then I'm going back up to Boston. I wanted to let you know what was going on. I'll call you later and let you know what the arrangements are."

"Okay son, please give them my sympathy."

"Talk to you later, Dad."

Chapter 46

Susanna and Mrs. O'Hara were up early and had finished packing. They had loaded up the car and were now cleaning up after breakfast. Susanna had tried for over an hour to get a hold of John to no avail. His office receptionist told her that he had not come in and had informed them that he would be gone for a couple of days. He did say, however, that he would check in with them for messages, and the receptionist asked if she would like to leave one. She asked to please have him call her on her cell phone.

"Mrs. O'Hara, let me try one more time before we leave."

Susanna picked up the telephone and tried to reach John again. There was no answer at home, and she left a final voice mail message.

"I guess we better get going, I'm sure Quincy will be happy to see us."

They made sure everything was closed up and locked. Mrs. O'Hara went out the door first and went to her car. Susanna followed and locked the door behind her. She went to the Durango and made sure that everything would be comfy for

Quincy for the ride home. She then gave a final look at the house. She pulled out first and Mrs. O'Hara followed her to the vet.

Dr. Marlow knew they were coming and was waiting for them.

"Hi, Ms. Smith, Mrs. O'Hara. Quincy is waiting for you. Come on back."

They went to the back room and sitting on a mat waiting impatiently was Quincy. Seeing Susanna and Mrs. O'Hara, he stood up and started to wag his stubby tail. He was really looking so much better.

"Hi, Quincy, are you ready to go home? Look who's going home, too!"

Mrs. O'Hara went over to pet his head and ears. He was so happy to see both of them. Susanna put his collar and leash on and walked him very slowly out to the reception room.

"Ms. Smith, I recommend that you take Quincy to your vet at home as soon as you can. Have him contact me, and I will fax the records to him so he can see what we did. I think he's going to be fine. I've given him his pills for the morning but make sure he gets them this afternoon and before you go to bed tonight. Also, see to it he gets a lot of water as well. I think that's it. Take it slow going home. I'll help you get him into the car."

"Dr. Marlow, thank you for all your help. I'm glad you were here to help Quincy.

What do I owe you for your services?"

"The bill has been paid."

"Paid! By whom?" asked Susanna.

"John Shaw came by this morning and took care of the bill. He made me promise not to accept any money from you. He said it was the least he could do."

"When was he here?"

"He came in around eight-thirty and left right after paying the bill."

"Thank you, Dr. Marlow. I'll have to call him."

Susanna walked Quincy a little bit before she went to the car. He was slower, but seemed to be perking up more each day. Dr. Marlow then helped her get Quincy into the car and comfortably situated.

"Goodbye both of you. Have a safe trip home."

Susanna and Mrs. O'Hara watched Dr. Marlow go back into the clinic. Standing by the Durango, she looked at Mrs. O'Hara.

"With everything that happened last night he still came by to take care of the bill. He really is a good man isn't he?" said Susanna.

"Yes he is, Darlin'."

"We better get to Mr. Shaw's office. I need to give him the keys. We also need to say goodbye. Follow me, Mrs. O'Hara.

Chapter 47

Mrs. O'Hara was duly impressed by William Shaw's office. Upon hearing that they were in the reception room and wanted to see him, he personally came out to greet them.

"Margaret, Susanna, please come into the office and sit down."

"William, what a beautiful place—it's grand! You must really enjoy working here."

"Mr. Shaw, how is John? I've tried to reach him and keep getting no answer. I know he went by Dr. Marlow's this morning. We must have just missed him. Do you know where I might reach him?" inquired Susanna.

"He was here a little after nine. He had been up in Boston with Jerry's family. He said it was a bad night. John was going home to clean up and then go back up to Boston to help Jerry's mom with the funeral arrangements. He might still be at home if you want to try him there. Here, let me call for you."

William Shaw dialed the number and waited for the connection. The phone rang six times and was finally picked up by voice mail.

"I'm sorry Susanna. He seems to be gone already."

"I left a message at his office and on his home voice mail, I hope he calls me. I wouldn't blame him if he didn't. Mr. Shaw, we can't stay too long, I have Quincy in the car and we need to get on our way. I just wanted to apologize to you for my behavior the other night. You were right, my Aunt Susanna would have been more understanding and forgiving. I hope I get the opportunity to right this wrong."

"Susanna, no apology is necessary. I knew you were upset, and the fact that you are trying to reach John is enough for me."

Susanna handed him the wooden box containing the letters. "I am leaving these letters in your care.

"Thank you for everything. The keys to the house are in this envelope. Please set up an account as we discussed for the upkeep. I trust your judgment.

"Oh, and would you also make sure to give John this envelope for me? You will see him before I do."

"I'll be happy to do all of this for you, and I will make it a point to reach John and give him the envelope as soon as I can," said William.

"Well, I think that's all for me. I'll say goodbye for now. I'll be in touch. Mrs. O'Hara, I'll meet you out by the car."

Susanna left the two of them in the office and went out to check on Quincy and wait. She knew Mrs. O'Hara wanted to say goodbye in private and respected her wishes.

"William, I'm sorry to be leaving. Thank you for all your help. I'll miss you. 'Tis a long time since I've had the company of a fine man, such as yourself. Susanna will be back, she just doesn't know it yet. The ties here are too strong. When she does I'll come back to visit again."

"Margaret, would you ever consider moving here? I would love to be able to see you. Do you have family in New Jersey?"

"No, my family is still in Ireland. William, all I can tell you is that I will think about it."

"Good, at least the door is not closed. I have that to hold on to."

"I must go, Susanna and Quincy are waiting. Goodbye William."

William got up and kissed her on the cheek. He walked her to the front door of the office and watched her go. But he knew in his heart of hearts that he would see her again. He really liked Margaret and never thought he could feel this kind of kinship again, especially after Susanna passed away.

"I'll give her a little time and call her," he thought.

Back in his office, he saw the envelope on his desk and made a mental note to give John another call later.

Chapter 48

John went directly home after visiting his father. He took a shower, packed some clean clothes and a suit to take to Boston.

He walked out the door and as it closed behind him he heard the telephone ringing.

"I wonder if I should get that," he hesitated.

"I'll check the messages later. I need to get going."

He knew this trip to Boston would be the hardest one he'd ever have to take.

Chapter 49

"John, I'm glad that's over. It was all very sad. I hope the police catch whoever did this. I think it would give Jerry's family closure."

They were sitting in William's library at home. It was Tuesday evening and the funeral had been held earlier in the day. It had been a long five days.

"Me too, Dad!"

"John, I waited until the funeral was over to talk to you about Susanna."

"I didn't get her message until after she had gone home to New Jersey. It wouldn't have done any good anyway."

"She came to see me before she left. She left the letters in my care, and I'm going to take care of the house for her in her absence. She was very anxious to speak to you and was very upset when she couldn't reach you. I think you're wrong. I think she cares for you very much. She asked me to give you this."

William handed over the envelope to John that Susanna had left in his care.

"What's this?" queried John.

"I don't know, but I told her I would make sure you got it. Do you want me to leave you alone?"

"No, Dad. I'm really beat. I think I'll take this home and read it there. I'll talk to you tomorrow. Goodnight, Dad."

As John was walking out the door, William stopped him.

"John, whatever's in that envelope, I'm here if you need me. I love you son. You did the right thing."

"Thanks, Dad. I love you too."

When he was alone, William Shaw thought his son had been through enough. He hoped whatever Susanna wrote to him wouldn't add to his burden. Tired after a long day, he decided to have a brandy and read his book before going to bed.

Chapter 50

As he sat in his chair at home, John traced the outline of the envelope in his hand. He was debating whether to open it or not. He knew he had to but was afraid he would not like what was inside. Taking a deep breath, he slit the top with a letter opener and took out the two handwritten pages. The first thing he noticed was the beauty of the handwriting. The next was the greeting.

June 3, 2004

Dear John,

I'm sorry I couldn't reach you before I left for New Jersey. I have so much to say and would like to have told you face to face. I will have to depend on this method of conveyance as did my ancestor, Abigail Adams.

Since coming to Weymouth and the ensuing time spent there, I learned a lot about myself. The history of my family and the remarkable life of my Aunt Susanna made me take a second look at how I'm living my own life.

They were wonderful role models and I'm ashamed to say I don't come up to their standards. John, I've been very unkind to you and, what's more, very unforgiving. You were there from the very beginning to help. The break-in was hard to take, but when Quincy got shot and I thought I would lose him, I really was beside myself. I was too busy looking for someone to blame. Unfortunately, I took it out on you. I think I was so stubborn about this because I felt guilty, guilty that I put everyone in harm's way by being so careless. The truth is that no one was responsible but Jerry Carter.

You, your father and Mary Connor have all made me feel welcome and Mrs. O'Hara has been my surrogate mother. Family and friends are the most important things in the world. For me to turn on you is unconscionable. Even when Jerry Carter was brutally murdered you accepted responsibility and helped his family. You are a good friend, John Shaw. Thank you for being there when I needed you.

I'm going to ask you for a big favor. If you can't do this, I will understand. John, please forgive me. I would like us to remain friends. I would really like to see you again. If, after all I've said or done, this is impossible, I will respect your decision.

Quincy is much improved and your quick action is what saved his life. Even then, all I could do was stand like a frozen statue. I'm taking him home because I believe he will heal better in familiar surroundings. I know he likes you and I'm sure he will miss having you around.

For the first time, thanks to my Aunt Susanna, I can finally do what I've always wanted to do: go back to school and get my doctorate. I've wanted to teach like my father and can now go after that goal. I'm thinking of going to Boston College. If I do, I will settle things in New Jersey and move to Weymouth. Would it make you uncomfortable to have me living there? I will find another University if you are.

Please call me, or write me if you prefer, to let me know how you feel. I would like a new beginning. I hope you do, too. If I don't hear from you, I will take your silence as an answer. If this is the last contact we have, then know, John Shaw, that I will always have a warm spot in my heart for you.

Yours,
Susanna
P.S. Thank you for what you did at Dr. Marlow's.

THE BEGINNING

CHAPTER NOTES

CHAPTER 2

1. http:// takusus.com/architecture/1colonial.html. This website referred to the architecture in New England during this historical period. It states that the houses were built with a design that was fashioned after medieval architecture. This website further explains that homes in New England were copied after the homes in Great Britain.

CHAPTER 3

2. http://www.weymouth.ma.us/history/index.asp.

CHAPTER 4

On page 27 reference is made to a plat. A plat is a real estate term and refers to a map, or plan of a piece of land.

CHAPTER 5

3. L. H. Butterfield et al., eds., The Book of Abigail and John: Selected Letters of the Adams Family 1762-1784 (Cambridge: 1975) pages 83-84.

4. John Mack Farragher, ed., The American Heritage Encyclopedia of American History (New York: 1998) page 4.

5. Ibid page 523.

CHAPTER 8

6. www.galegroup.com/free
7. Ibid
8. Ibid
9. Ibid
10. Ibid
11. Ibid
12. Ibid
13. Ibid
14. Ibid
15. Edith B. Gelles, Portia: The World of Abigail Adams (Bloomington: 1992) Page 31.

CHAPTER 9

16. L. H. Butterfield et al., eds., The Book of Abigail and John: Selected Letters of the Adams Family 1762-1784 (Cambridge: 1975) pages 84-86.

(I.) This was the first of the inserts I made up in the letters. All of the future inserts will have (I) after it so that the reader will be able to know which was actual and which is original. The inserts set the storyline for Abigail to help solve and catch the murderer of Josiah Quincy.

CHAPTER 11

(I.) Second Insert. Setting the stage.
17. L. H. Butterfield et al., eds., The Book of Abigail and John: Selected Letters of the Adams Family 1762-1784 (Cambridge: 1975) pages 86-88.

CHAPTER 12

18. Lynne Withey, Dearest Friend: A Life of Abigail Adams (New York: 1981) pages 64-69.

CHAPTER 13

19. Greg Sukiennik, Park Chronicles Adams' Legacy. <u>The Sunday Star Ledger</u>. September 2, 2001, Page 6 Section Eight.

CHAPTER 15

(I.) Third Insert.
20. L. H. Butterfield et al., eds., The Book of Abigail and John: Selected Letters of the Adams Family 1762-1784 (Cambridge: 1975) pages 90-91.
(I.) Fourth Insert.
21. L. H. Butterfield et al., eds., The Book of Abigail and John: Selected Letters of the Adams Family 1762-1784 (Cambridge: 1975) pages 92-94.

CHAPTER 22

22. L.H. Butterfield et al., eds., The Book of Abigail and John: Selected Letters of the Adams Family 1762-1784 (Cambridge: 1975) pages 97-99.
(I.) Fifth Insert.
23. L. H. Butterfield et al., eds., The Book of Abigail and John: Selected Letters of the Adams Family 1762-1784 (Cambridge: 1975) pages 99-104.

CHAPTER 36

24. L. H. Butterfield et al., eds., The Book of Abigail and John: Selected Letters of the Adams Family 1762-1784 (Cambridge: 1975) page 106.

25. Ibid pages 106-107.

26. Ibid page 107.

27. Ibid page 108.

(I.) This is the last Insert. This ties up all the loose ends and solves the mystery of the death of Josiah Quincy.

28. L.H. Butterfield et al., eds., The Book of Abigail and John: Selected Letters of the Adams Family 1762-1784 (Cambridge: 1975) pages 112-114.

CHAPTER 37

29. L.H. Butterfield et al., eds., The Book of Abigail and John: Selected Letters of the Adams Family 1762-1784 (Cambridge: 1975) page 81.

30. Ibid page 82.

31. Ibid page 82.

32. Ibid page 88.

33. Ibid pages 106-108.

34. Ibid pages 108-110.

BIBLIOGRAPHY

Adams, Charles, Francis, ed. *The Familiar Letters of John Adams and His Wife Abigail Adams during the Revolution.* New York: Hurd & Houghton, 1876.

Anthony, Carl, Sferrazza. *First Ladies The Saga of the Presidents' Wives And Their Power 1789-1961.* New York: Quill, William Morrow, 1990.

Bober, Natalie S. *Abigail Adams Witness To A Revolution.* New York: Aladdin Paperbacks, 1998.

Bowen, Cathrine Drinker. *John Adams and the American Revolution.* Boston: Little, Brown, and Co., 1933.

Butterfield, L.H., Marc Friedlaender, and Mary-Jo Line. eds. *The Book of Abigail and John: Selected Letters of the Adams Family 1762-1784.* Cambridge Mass.: Harvard University Press, 1975.

Cappon, Lester J., ed. *The Adams-Jefferson Letters.* Chapel Hill, N.C.: University of North Carolina Press, 1987.

Carruth, Gorton, & Eugene Ehrlich. eds. *American Quotations.* New York: Portland House, 1988.

Ellis, Joseph J. *Founding Brothers The Revolutionary Generation.* New York: Alfred A. Knopf, 2000.

Faragher, John Mack. ed. *The American Heritage Encyclopedia of American History.* New York: Henry Holt and Company, 1998.

Ferling, John. *John Adams A Life.* New York: Henry Holt and Company, 1992.

Foss, William O. ed. *First Ladies Quotation Book.* New York: Barricade Books, Inc. 1999.

Gelles, Edith B. *Portia: The World of Abigail Adams.* Bloomington and Indianapolis: Indiana University Press, 1992.

Gould, Lewis L. ed. *American First Ladies-Their Lives and Their Legacy.* New York & London: Garland Publishing, Inc., 1996.

McCullough, David. *John Adams.* New York: Simon and Schuster, 2001.

Mintz, Steven and Susan Kellogg. eds. *Domestic Revolutions- A Social History of American Family Life.* New York: The Free Press, 1988.

Nagel, Paul C. *Descent from Glory-Four Generations of the John Adams Family.* Massachusetts and England: Harvard University Press, 1983.

Nicholas, Anna Katherine. *Weimaraners.* New Jersey: T.F.H. Publications, 1990.

Roberts, Cokie. *Founding Mothers.* New York: Harper Collins Publishers Inc., 2004

Spalding, Matthew. ed. *The Founders' Almanac.* Washington, D.C.: The Heritage Foundation , 2001.

Thompson, C. Bradley. *John Adams and the Spirit of Liberty.* Kansas: University Press of Kansas, 1998.

Withey, Lynne. *Dearest Friend: A Life of Abigail Adams.* New York: Free Press, 1981.

INTERNET SOURCES

http://www.galegroup.com/free_resources/whm/bio/adams_a.htm
http://www.ttrotsky.pwp.blueyonder.co.uk/tech/poison.htm
http://www.abigailadams.org/The_Birthplace/the_birthplace.html
http://www.whitehouse.gov/history/firstladies/aa2.html
http://www.womenshistory.about.com/library/bio/bl1st_adams_abigail.htm
http://www.umkc.edu/imc/adamssa.htm
http://www.masshist.org/apgenealogy.html
http://www.masshist.org/apbios.html
http://www.masshist.org/aptimeline.html
http://www.masshist.org/apquotes.html
http://www.earlyamerica.com/earlyamerica/notable/adamsa/indes.html
http://www.abigailadams.org/Abigail/abigail.html
http://www.key-biz.com/ssn/Weymouth/esker_park.html
http://www.key-biz.com/ssn/Weymouth/history.html
http://www.weymouth.mass.info/online/portal.aspx
http://www.weymouth.ma.us/history/index.asp
http://www.tuckertonseaport.org/saltbox.html
http://www.johnstonhousehmb.org/
http://www.takus.com/architecture/1colonial.html
http://www.fiddlergreen.net/buildings/new-england/saltbox/hse.htm
http://www.artists4psp.com/karren/salt/salt.html
http://www.nps.gov/adam

NEWSPAPERS

Sukiennik, Greg. "Park Chronicles Adams' Legacy." <u>The Sunday Star Ledger</u> 2 September 2001. Page 6 Section Eight.

Unknown. "Abigail Adams: A Woman Ahead Of Her Time." <u>The Quincy Sun</u> 3 July 2002. Page 10A.

DICTIONARY

Webster's New World Dictionary of the American Language. Cleveland and New York: The World Publishing Company, 1968.